Jerry Piasecki is the author of 13 published novels for young readers. His background includes over 15 years with the United Nations, including work in the areas of humanitarian affairs, women's empowerment, children's rights, and UN Radio News. His novel *Marie in the Shadow of the Lion* was the first novel ever to be published by the United Nations.

For over 25 years, he worked as a broadcast journalist internationally, as well as in New York and Detroit. His experience includes 14 years as the creative director at a mid-sized advertising/marketing agency.

Jerry has one daughter, Amanda; and two grandsons, Ben and Harry. He and his wife, Wendy Rollin, currently live in Connecticut and Michigan with their Boston Terrier, Tima.

To my daughter, Amanda, who loved and was so loved by her
Grandma Lucy.
To my sister, Carole, who lived the story with me.
To my darling Wendy, without whom this book never could have
or would have been written.
And to Harry and Lucy – Thank you. Love you forever.

Jerry Piasecki

HARRY AND LUCY

AUSTIN MACAULEY PUBLISHERS™

LONDON • CAMBRIDGE • NEW YORK • SHARJAH

Ordering Information:
Quantity sales: special discounts are available on quantity purchases by corporations, associations, and others. For details, contact the publisher at the address below.

Publisher's Cataloging-in-Publication data
Piasecki, Jerry
Harry and Lucy

ISBN 9781643781259 (Paperback)
ISBN 9781643781266 (Hardback)
ISBN 9781643781273 (E-Book)

The main category of the book — Fiction / Romance / Historical / General

www.austinmacauley.com/us

First Published (2019)
Austin Macauley Publishers LLC
40 Wall Street, 28th Floor
New York, NY 10005
USA

mail-usa@austinmacauley.com
+1 (646) 5125767

Preface

The following is a work of fiction.
The stories of the lives of Harry and Lucy are true.

Prologue

Do you think there's a reason why certain people come together? Why do you like the sound of one person's voice but wince at the tone of another's? Why do some people smell good and others kind of go the other way? Several women have told me they know from the moment they meet a man whether or not they will go to bed with him. Sex at first sight? Why? Why do men view some guys as rivals or enemies and others as life-long buddies and brothers? Why do some people fall in love? I mean really in love. Forever. For always. For better or worse. Until death do they part?

Why do we go on living after those we love die? Or do we? Certainly, the moment someone leaves us, the second they pass, we are no longer living in quite the same way as before. Yeah, the sun rises, we go to work, and sleep comes; although, perhaps, not quite as gently on all counts. The world still bursts with color. Reds, blues, greens, and yellows persist in making their vivid statements. But like all colors, they are subject to shades of individual perception and interpretation. We believe these colors are real, even though they are perceived differently by each person.

Our world is blurred by the passing of our present into our past, but we remain ever resolute that what we recognize as real is nonetheless so; that the table in the kitchen remains the table in the kitchen, not just a bunch of atoms spinning wildly with divine precision to create an illusion we can all grasp and hold on to. The beliefs we all share, a chair is a chair, continue, but our lives change when someone so familiar, so taken for granted, so loved, is lost. The person who ate at the table and sat on that chair is awkwardly absent from the scene; a scene not quite as familiar or comforting as it had been the day before. The person we once held, who touched our hair and called our name is gone…just out of reach.

Memories linger, then languish until they are gone or transformed into memories of themselves. When can you no longer hear his voice or feel her fingers? When does the sound of their laughter fade? When do their scents disappear from the clothing we keep in their memory? The lives we knew when we were with them are over, or perhaps they are never really at an end. Nothing is less solid and more temporary than what we define as 'reality'. It can change in the blink of an eye, a baby's first cry or a darling's last breath. I don't know the answers...but at least now I know what I believe.

This is a love story.

Chapter 1

Beemans gum. That's how it all started, with a stick of Beemans gum. A penny a stick; a hefty price back then.

Hunger, humiliation, and death had been part of Harry Piasecki's life from a very young age. It was the Great Depression, and he and his friends had to crawl over barbed wire on the top of fences to steal coal from the railroad yard to keep their families from freezing in the judgmental and unjust Michigan winter. Anyone caught was beaten senseless by the railroad guard who was usually, actually always, drunk and often invited his boozed-up buddies to join in the fun. The guard and his pals would laugh and swear in Polish, as they kicked with heavy leather boots and swung their nightsticks with all their might. None of the victims would go to a hospital. Hospitals were for rich people. These boys either crawled home and recovered or didn't and were forgotten.

Back then, Hamtramck, Michigan was predominately Polish—a famished Eastern European ghetto girdled entirely by the City of Detroit. It was filled with people from places like Lublin, Znin, Trzchianka, Szadek, Szczebrzesyn, Krakow, and Warsaw. All had come in search of full bellies and better lives in that land of milk and money—America. Living in Hamtramck, they either kept their dreams or lost all hope.

Harry had seen his six-month-old brother, Mikey, die from diphtheria. He was buried in the family's tiny backyard near the fence bordering the stone-covered alley. Funerals were also for rich people. A sister, who never had a name, died shortly after being born at home. His parents had no money for a doctor, and the neighbor lady who had promised to help with the delivery was visiting a friend that day. Harry's mother almost bled to death while holding her dead daughter in her arms. After that, she started to pray a lot and to drink even more.

Food was scarce, and malnutrition was a given for many. Harry knew what it felt like to go to bed hungry and with the knowledge that the next night would be the same. But when sleep finally overcame the gnawing in his belly, Harry would dream of getting fat. He would dream of being warm. He would dream of being happy. He would dream of finding his love.

Harry never told his dad about those dreams, in fact, he tried to talk to him as little as possible. His father most often dealt with his kids from one end of a heavy, brown, worn-leather, shaving strap made for sharpening straight razors. The kids would feel the sting from the other end on their buttocks, backs, arms, wherever the swing happened to hit. All six of Harry's surviving brothers and sisters had felt it to the point of familiarity. They had learned how to duck and turn in a way that would have the strap land in places less painful or humiliating.

Any violation of Felix Piasecki's rules would result in a beating. If one of the girls stayed out until after dark, she would be greeted by the strap as soon as she walked in the front door. If one of the boys ever lost a fight, the beating at home would be far worse than any injury inflicted on the street. That's how Felix had been raised by his father back in Poland. He continued the tradition so that his girls would learn to listen, and his boys would grow tough. It made Harry keep his mouth shut. It also made him angry.

Felix Piasecki hadn't had a dream he could remember in 20 years.

If Felix ever found out about the Beemans gum, that his son was 'throwing good money away' and keeping food off the table, because of some girl, Harry knew he would get the beating of his life...or maybe of his death. But to 16-year-old Harry Piasecki, that Beemans gum was worth every penny and any risk. He would walk twenty and a half blocks every day to buy a stick of that gum from a 14-year-old girl named Lucy Buraczynski. Her father owned a one-room candy/animal feed/beer store on the east side of Hamtramck. That's where Harry and Lucy fell in love. That was a long time ago.

# # #

"I wish I could go with you," Lucy Piasecki said softly into the 'bad' phone that was beside her couch in the assisted living apartment. The 'good' phone was in the bedroom, but getting up from her corner of the sofa and using the walker to reach it before voicemail picked up was a race she could no longer hope to win. The broken hip saw to that.

"God, I haven't been to Petoskey in 30 years at least. Last time was with Uncle Louie, when Mary died."

Lucy's son, Jerry, shifted the phone restlessly from his right ear to his left. He knew that telling his mom his plans to travel to Petoskey, Michigan, a place the Piaseckis had visited many times as a young family was not going to be an easy conversation. "I know, Mom. I can't wait to see it again. I wonder if it's changed much."

"Are you driving all the way from New York by yourself?"

"No, remember Rob, Mom?"

"He plays guitar," Lucy said recalling how Jerry's friend, Rob, had once played Glen Miller's song *'String of Pearls'* for her, on his guitar, in the hospital when she was recovering from her hip surgery. She didn't think he played it very well, but she appreciated the effort.

"Yeah, that's him. Well, Rob is going to be coming with me for company."

"Well, I'm glad you're not making the drive alone. Still I wish I could go with you. The last time I was there was when Mary died. I drove up with Uncle Louie."

Jerry first met his friend Rob when he took a job at a radio station in White Plains, New York. WFAS prided itself on being the 'Voice of Westchester', which for many years it was, particularly on snowy mornings when it seemed as though every student in the county would call to ask if their school was closed. Jerry was an aggressive reporter; Rob a laid back engineer.

The two became almost instant friends for life, although neither one was sure why. Maybe Jerry motivated Rob, and Rob slowed Jerry down. Maybe it was none of those things, but the friendship stuck and the two men actually shared an apartment for a year near the station, and later, a house in Mt

Kisco, New York until Jerry moved back to Detroit to work at a bigger station in a much bigger radio market.

Before moving in with Rob, Jerry had stayed with his sister Anne, who lived in Ridgefield, Connecticut which is just across the state line from northern Westchester County New York. Anne had married successfully and had given up a promising stage career decades earlier. She was happy with her choices. Jerry's past marriages and choices had been somewhat less successful.

When Anne and Jerry were children, they would spend summers in Petoskey with their mom and dad, Harry and Lucy.

Petoskey, a city of around 6,000 permanent residents and at least three or four times that many visitors in the summer and winter, sits on the pinkie side of the ring finger in the mitten that is the lower peninsula of Michigan. Anyone from the state will happily point to their hometowns by lifting a hand and pointing to the exact spot on the mitten where they were raised.

Driving in from the south on Rt. 131, Petoskey comes into view as you crest a hill and look down at the shimmering waters of Lake Michigan's Little Traverse Bay. It is a magical sight, millions of tiny sparkling loose diamonds dancing in the sunlight on soft turquoise waves, welcoming you to a world not ruled by what we perceive, but by what exists when we blink. Petoskey is an Odawa nation word for 'where the light shines through the clouds'.

Fifty years ago when Jerry was only seven years old and Anne 11, there were fewer people and a lot fewer hotels, but the awe-inspiring vision, when coming over the hill, was always the same.

# # #

Lucy broke her hip while making stuffed peppers. One step back in her narrow kitchen, one loose rug, one fall; one life forever changed. We all have a moment when the end begins. That was hers.

Lucy lived in the small, two-bedroom apartment in Ridgefield, Connecticut, for about five years. Jerry's move to New York had pulled her from the comfort of her life-long home in Detroit. (Below the outside of the thumb and about an

14

inch or so above the wrist) The apartment was the first place where she had ever lived alone. It was *her* apartment, Lucy's place, and she loved it.

# # #

While Jerry and Rob often didn't see each other for years after the WFAS days, each time they did manage to get together it seemed like only a day had passed. It was that kind of friendship. Both were now divorced; Rob from a Russian lawyer named Tatiana, and Jerry from an American lesbian named Lydia. Jerry didn't know of his wife's orientation until six years and one child had been shared between them. Rob knew from the start that his bride was both Russian and a lawyer, but he said "I do" anyway. Opposing the will of Tatiana would have taken just too much energy and didn't seem worth the trouble of it all.

Jerry lived in Michigan while raising his daughter until she moved off to college. In her junior year, he headed back east after being hired to try to 'turn United Nations Radio into a more professional broadcast operation'. Jerry liked to describe the job as 'mission impossible' in all six official UN languages. Rob, meanwhile, now taught and did radio engineering at Westchester Community College just north of New York City.

When they were younger, both men had talked about taking road trips together. Back then, they had only managed one such adventure to Maine. Now, with more time and fewer wives, they were pretty much free to travel as they liked.

One day Jerry called his friend. "Hey, man, road trip?"

"Sure, I have some vacation time saved up. Where to, Jer?"

Jerry hadn't planned a destination when he made the call. But when Rob asked his question, Jerry immediately answered, "How about Petoskey?"

# # #

"Will you see your Aunt Mary while you're in Petoskey?"

Jerry held his breath for a second. Lucy's dementia had been getting worse by the week, if not by the day. He didn't know what to say.

"Mom, Mary died a long time ago, remember? You went to the funeral with Louie."

"Of course I remember," Lucy always tried to cover what she called her 'lapses'. In her 30s, she had joked about hoping to either 'die quickly or decompose with dignity'. Neither wish had been granted.

"I know you do, Mom. You must have meant Mary's kids, remember Bobby and Billy?"

Everyone always tried to support Lucy in these moments. The conscious goal was to help her avoid embarrassment. Sometimes it worked, other times it was patronizing.

"I bet they still live in that old house on Mitchell Street," Jerry said in a voice too cheery and with a smile too broad. "I'll take a picture if it's still there."

"Jerry, of course I remember Bobby and Billy," Lucy said, her voice dropped to a whisper. "But actually, for what it's worth, I really did mean Mary."

"Mom, please."

"You never know about Petoskey," Lucy said softly.

"What do you mean?" Jerry asked.

Lucy looked at Harry's army picture on her TV set. She thought of something he had told her many years ago, something that happened in the bar just outside of Petoskey where he worked for a summer to see what it would be like to live Up North. Harry wanted to jump at the chance to move. He dreamed of owning The Hub Bar on Crooked Lake. Lucy didn't share his dream, so they stayed in Detroit.

"It's better for the kids in Detroit," she had told Harry. "Anne has all of her friends there, and Jerry has football. And your doctors are all there."

Harry listened to Lucy's arguments, knowing that what she wasn't saying was that she would miss her brothers and her friends. More than once that summer, Lucy had also expressed dread at being snowed under from November to early April.

Once Lucy completed her arguments, all Harry said was "Okay, sweetheart. Whatever you say."

It broke his heart to give up The Hub; it would have killed him to disappoint his darling Lucy. After that summer, Harry drove his family back to Detroit where he bought his second bar on 7 Mile Road. His first bar had simply been named 'Harry's'. He renamed the second one 'The 7 Mile Hub'.

What Harry had whispered to Lucy in bed after coming home from work at 3 a.m. in the soothing chill of an early Petoskey morning, had sounded crazy. Lucy knew her husband was anything but. She had never told anyone what Harry had said. He had made her swear she never would. The very thought of his words still made her shiver.

"Mom," Jerry said after several seconds of silence. "What did you mean; you never know about Petoskey?"

"I should never have brought it up," Lucy said quickly into the telephone, "Forget it."

Jerry heard the telephone fall against the coffee table. Now from a distance, he heard his mom shout, "Darn it. Hang on, Jerry, I dropped the phone."

# # #

From the day they met in that candy/feed/beer store on Conant Street, a few blocks south of Caniff on the east side of Hamtramck, Lucy never forgot the unique pungent minty scent of Beemans gum on Harry's breath. In her mind, she could always envision the moment that this skinny redheaded teenager with a tough-guy stare and angelic smile had walked into the store for the first time.

Harry had been stopped in his tracks the instant he had stepped through the door of that store by what he later told his brother Reds (Joseph) was 'the most beautiful girl in the world'.

"She won't even look at you," Reds had said. "You're from different sides of the tracks. Plus, you're ugly like a son of a bitch, and you smell like shit."

The second half of Reds' statement was part of an on-going joke between brothers. The part about 'the tracks' was true.

"She'll look at me alright," Harry said with a mischievous grin. "She'll not only look at me, she'll marry me."

"You're not only ugly and shitty, you're also fucking nuts."

"We'll see," Harry laughed. "Asshole."

Every day, except for Sunday when the store was closed and Lucy was in St. Florian church with her parents, Harry would show up at one point or another. He would casually look around at the various candies, pretending he was trying to decide which one to buy. He'd then put the penny he had earned, borrowed, found, or pilfered from his father's pocket, on the counter and order a stick of gum. Exactly when he got that penny determined what time Harry could head to the store. But he always made sure he did get it because that penny was his excuse and his ticket to talk to the 'most beautiful girl in the world'.

The ritual became a daily routine with talking turning to flirtation and flirtation to infatuation.

Harry would laugh about his having the 'Sweetest breath in Hamtramck' before blowing her a kiss.

Lucy would turn red with embarrassment and secretly take in the scent. To her, he didn't just have the sweetest breath in Hamtramck; he had the sweetest breath in the world.

Many years later, she smelled the cherished fragrance one final time when Harry took his last breath.

# # #

"So when will you and Rob be going?" Lucy's voice came back strong and steady over the phone. It was now tinged with a bit of annoyance. "I sure wish I could go with you. I haven't been to Petoskey in 30 years at least. Last time I went was with Uncle Louie, when Mary died."

"I know, Mom," Jerry said sadly. "We're going to drive out on Tuesday."

"That's the tenth, right?"

"Yeah, I think so, why?"

"And you're going to stay for a week?"

"Yeah, that's the plan."

"So, you'll be there on the 14th."

"Yeah, but I don't understand, Mom. What's the big deal about the 14th?"

"You'll see."

"See what, Mom? You're kind of freaking me out."

"Just forget it. I'm just getting old. Sometimes, I really don't know what I'm talking about."

This was not one of those times.

#

Harry Piasecki was only 56 years old when he died in the suburban Detroit nursing home where he was sent after his third major stroke, the one that had put him in a coma and made it impossible for Lucy to take care of him at home. She wrote on a piece of scrap paper from the nursing station on the day he was admitted: *'Doctors hold no hope. Harry unable to move at all—not even fingers or toes.'*

One of the home's doctors told Lucy that he was 'brain dead'. Another, a man who happened to also be a long-time close family friend said: "Lucy, it's really not Harry anymore."

The strokes were caused by a congenital brain tumor that was activated when his head slammed onto the floor of the B29 bomber he served on as a gunner in World War II. The Japanese Zero that caused the bomber pilot to bank swiftly to the right never fired a shot. With today's technology, Harry's condition could be dealt with through relatively routine laser surgery. Back then, it was a death sentence.

For exactly three months, Lucy would go to that nursing home every day to hold her husband's hand.

#

Eighteen year old Harry gently held Lucy's hand as they slowly skated around the roller rink where they would go every Saturday after they had started 'dating'. Neither was a particularly good skater, but both had fun holding each other's hand to stay upright. They both knew skating was just an excuse to touch, but in 1941 excuses were necessary.

On this particular Saturday, Lucy had tried to cut quickly in front of Harry when she lost control of her skates and actually went airborne. Harry had to release her hand and pull her body close in order to prevent her from tumbling hard onto the shining wood floor. They looked into each other's eyes for a moment before starting to laugh, but they didn't pull away. While the laughter faded, they remained lost in each other's eyes, in each other's arms. That was the first time they kissed.

"Will you always be there to catch me?" Lucy put her head ever so gently against Harry's chest.

"Always."

# # #

"I'll be loving you, always. With a love that's true, always," Lucy whispered the words as she sang into Harry's ear at the nursing home. She did it every day, never knowing if he heard her, or felt her tears fall onto his cheek. Then one sunny Detroit morning in early May, Lucy sang the song for the last time. "Not for just an hour. Not for just a day. Not for just a year, but always…always."

That morning, for just a split second before he died, Harry partially opened his eyes. They glistened with what had been hidden tears. He looked at Lucy and smiled softly. He moved his lips and oh so gently sighed, "Always."

When his eyes closed, for just a passing second, Lucy felt embraced by the youthful minty fragrance of Beemans gum.

Chapter 2

Jerry and Rob decided to take Jerry's red Jeep to Petoskey for one very good reason: Rob's 21-year-old Fiat Spider had no real floor to speak of on the passenger side. If you rode with Rob, you needed to keep your feet up on the dashboard. If you looked down you could actually watch the highway, and whatever was on it, zooming by below. Rob had named his beloved car Arlo.

The first time Jerry rode with Rob he had pointed out this slight deficiency, "Ah, Rob?" he said. "Have you noticed something about your car?"

"What's that Jer?"

"There's no fucking floor."

Rob had simply shrugged his shoulders and shifted into third gear.

"I can see Broadway down there."

Rob just starting happily humming *'On the Road Again'* as he shifted up to fourth and then fifth gear.

Jerry pressed his sneakered feet hard against the glove compartment. "What the hell happened to the floor?"

"New York City," Rob said matter-of-factly. "I think someone took it."

The truth is, the floor rusted out from wear and winter driving. A big chunk of it just kind of fell on to the road five miles outside Stockbridge Massachusetts about ten years ago. Rob never got around to getting it fixed, figuring it didn't really matter much back then, and it particularly didn't matter now that he was single again.

His ex, Tatiana, had taken her car and their Boston Terrier, Grisha, with her when she left. Rob couldn't care less about the BMW, but he really loved that dog.

Jerry and Rob headed out for Petoskey from New York City just before the sun turned darkness to day. New Jersey flew by quickly with Jerry pointing down at Rob's feet and extolling the virtues of having a car with a floor. Pennsylvania, however, seemed endless as they rolled mile after tedious mile toward Ohio.

Both Rob and Jerry had long since stopped commenting on, or even really noticing some gorgeous scenic valley or lush green mountain top. They stopped talking about their ex-wives or possible future girlfriends. They even turned off the radio after one local evangelist came on and promised to provide anyone in his fleeced flock with a 'full color picture of our lord Jesus Christ, signed by the big fellah personally hisself', in exchange for a 50-dollar donation.

The devout could get an unsigned picture for 25 dollars, but would not get the soul-saving benefits of the signature of God. "The deeper ya dig into those pockets or purses the closer you are to being an apprentice of the Almighty! You never oughta want to risk the Lord saying to your soul: 'you're fired!'"

Jerry stretched his back, which had started to ache somewhere between Lewisburg and Lock Haven PA.

"Well, at least, we can be thankful for one thing,"

Rob yawned, "And that would be what?"

"At least we're not driving through Texas. And, just think, in a few more hours..." Jerry let his statement drift.

"In a few hours what?" Rob bit the bait.

"We'll still be in fucking Pennsylvania."

By the time they finally reached Farmington Hills, a northern suburb of Detroit and the last place in Michigan Jerry had lived before moving to New York, Rob and Jerry felt as if they had driven in from Mars. This would be the stopping off point before the short, by comparison, four-hour ride to Petoskey the next day.

"I'm gonna crash out for a while," Rob said after they checked in at the Radisson Hotel just off 12 Mile Road. "What about you?"

While exhausted from the drive, Jerry also felt exhilarated being 'home'. He knew he wouldn't fall asleep until that day's assignments were complete.

"I think I'll take a little walk. I'll wake you in an hour to go for spareribs. You're going to love the Bone Yard!"

"You really want ribs today?" Rob had hoped to just pick up a Burger King or order in a pizza and call it a night.

"Yes," Jerry said without a moment's hesitation.

"Why, man?" Rob moaned.

"Have to. No choice."

Jerry rolled his suitcase toward the elevator. He would drop it off in his room before heading out. "Rob," he called back to his friend who was walking in the opposite direction. "What room are you in?"

Rob looked down at the magnetic card the receptionist had given him. He thought about lying so that Jerry couldn't find him, but instead tried the honest approach. "Room 126. But, just because you have to have ribs, don't I get a choice?"

"No."

Jerry knew he probably would never live in Michigan again, but the State and particularly the Detroit area would always be home. Jerry had moved to Farmington Hills from the east side of Detroit when his daughter, Amanda, was five. The need to relocate became crystal clear at about 2 a.m. one summer night when he woke up to find the air in his bedroom, and the whole house for that matter, aglow with a soft, shimmering, orange light.

Jumping out of bed, Jerry thought at first that the house was on fire and that he had to get Amanda to safety. But a quick glance out the window toward the alley revealed the true source of the eerie glow. Three large metal dumpsters and two garages were fully ablaze, with flames reaching 50 feet into the night sky and orange sparks floating up and disappearing amongst the stars.

"What's going on?" Jerry's mom, who had come to help take care of Amanda after her son's divorce, hurried into his room.

Jerry pointed to the window, "Look at the alley."

"Oh my God," Lucy whispered. "I'll call the fire department."

"Good," Jerry quickly put on his jeans and searched for his shoes. "I'm going to see what's happening back there."

"Be careful," Lucy said. "Maybe you should just stay inside until the firemen get here."

"Don't worry," Jerry slipped on his sneakers. "I'll be okay."

Before Lucy could stop him, Jerry was out the door and racing across the vacant lot next to his family's house toward the alley.

Lucy walked quickly to the phone, all the time muttering, "Just like your father."

"What the fuck are you doing?" Jerry shouted out to a young man who went only by the moniker 'Shotgun'.

Shotgun had moved into the neighborhood a few months earlier. The first time the two new neighbors met was in that same alley, which was now on fire. Shotgun had proudly shown Jerry the three bullet wound scars that formed a triangle from just to the right of his navel, down close to his pelvis and then up again.

"I got two more on my mother-fucking ass if you're interested."

"I'll pass," Jerry had said with a laugh. "I truly believe you, man."

"Cool," Shotgun had said. "You fucking better."

Shotgun was scarred and scary, even to those generally unaccustomed to fear. When the crack house gang on the corner had harassed Jerry and his daughter, Shotgun had said he'd take care of it. From then on, whenever the corner crack-heads saw Jerry and Amanda coming down the block, they would duck inside until they passed.

Sitting on Jerry's front porch having a beer, Jerry asked Shotgun what he had done.

"I told you I would take care of it, didn't I?" Shotgun slugged down the rest of his Stroh's beer and crushed the can. "You need to know more?"

"Nope," Jerry gave the right answer and the correct follow up. "Why don't I just get us another beer."

Shotgun smiled.

"I'm gonna find the motherfuckers that done this," Shotgun screamed as he ran down the alley past one of the burning garages. He held his .357 magnum revolver in one hand and a spiked baseball bat in the other.

"Some motherfucker is going to die. This is my neighborhood! You hear me, motherfuckers?" Shotgun shouted in to the darkness and the flames. "*My* fucking neighborhood!"

Jerry's first thought? *He's right.* His second? *Time to move.*

# # #

Harry and Lucy had purchased the small red brick colonial home on Packard Street, near 8 Mile Road, when Jerry was born. It was their dream house. A place, a nest, where they could raise their family and live as one. Back then, 8 Mile was out in the sticks.

# # #

As Rob sighed and accepted his fate, Jerry headed for the hotel exit. The warm and sticky late evening Michigan air brought back childhood memories of watering lawns, catching night crawlers with his dad for fishing and listening to Ernie Harwell calling Detroit Tigers games on a transistor radio.

Every night, as soon as the summer sun started to set, everyone in the neighborhood would take up their positions on the folding chairs, plastic-strip chaise lounges, or metal gliders the size of small couches that graced their porches or backyards.

Greetings, jokes, and gossip filled the thickening darkness. Words and laughter mixed and mingled with the aromas of cigarettes, cigars, cheap whiskey and usually galumpkis, pierogis, fresh kielbasa, or any manner of Polish delicacy that someone had cooked and consumed that evening.

Jerry still remembered each smell, each neighbor's name, and what their concrete porches felt like against his young-boy butt when he would visit them throughout the summer.

That was before air conditioning turned each house into a private bunker against the heat and human contact. Jerry and Anne had often talked about inventions and technical advancements made during their lifetimes that had changed the world in profound ways. Computers and the Internet always headed up the list, but air conditioning wasn't too far behind.

Now, as Jerry walked along 12 Mile Road in Farmington Hills, he felt embraced by the softness of familiarity and the comfort of history. He walked for a half hour through memories both vague and vivid. Then, in his mind, he heard a soft comforting voice from the past say the word that would always wake him up and make his mouth water. It was his mom's voice calling up the stairs to her sleeping children: "Ribs."

Years ago, those gentle summons would result in Jerry and Anne leaping from their beds with profound joy and almost vicious glee. On this night, on 12 Mile Road, it made Jerry smile broadly and reverse his course back toward the hotel. "Coming, Mom," he laughed out loud. "Coming!"

When he turned around, Jerry felt shadows slam into him from all sides. Something moved in the bushes to the right. A car honked its horn at nothing. He instinctively backed away from the swirling air that engulfed him. Then, as quickly and surprisingly, it was just night again. A calm, clammy southern Michigan summer night.

"Just the wind," Jerry said, walking quickly back toward the hotel.

Did a shadow duck behind the tree to his left? *Someone's watching me*, Jerry thought. *No, someone's calling me.*

# # #

"Full slab of ribs and a diet coke, please," Jerry happily placed his order with the teenaged Bone Yard Restaurant waitress, who seemed a bit concerned over her customer's unusually intense pleasure with his dinner selection. Jerry closed his menu and his eyes. Now he *really* felt like he was home.

Rob, who was still half asleep from his nap, just shook his head and shrugged his shoulders. "The guy likes his ribs," he explained to the increasingly befuddled waitress.

Jerry inhaled deeply, taking in the scent of meat and grease.

"He's also a little nuts," Rob smiled up at the waitress who took two steps back from the table.

"And what will you have?" she asked Rob.

"He'll have what I'm having," Jerry spoke just above a whisper.

Rob shrugged again and threw his hands up. "OK. Shouldn't argue with a crazy person, right?"

The waitress left the table as quickly as possible.

"Man, this is so cool." Jerry kept his eyes closed.

"Ahhhhh huh," Rob paused before asking the obvious question; "Would you like to tell me why?"

# # #

"Anne, Jerry: ribs." The 3 a.m. call from Lucy rang out loud and clear to Jerry and his sister. While Lucy spoke softly and gently on these occasions so as not to startle her sleeping children, Jerry and Anne would always sit bolt upright in their beds at the very whisper of that magic word. The thick unmistakable aroma of barbecue spareribs and fried potatoes filled the house. To Jerry and Anne, it was a heavenly scent because it meant that their father was home.

Once Harry and Lucy bought their first bar on 7 Mile Road, Harry rarely saw his children. He was asleep when they left for school and was out the door at 11 a.m. to pick up liquor and other supplies.

The family ate dinner at exactly 3:30 in the afternoon. Harry was off to work no later than 4 p.m. That was the schedule 6 days a week, 52 weeks a year. Because of Michigan blue laws, the bar couldn't officially sell alcohol on Sundays, but regular customers would be served their 'usual' behind locked and guarded doors.

After closing time on Saturday mornings, Harry would often stop and pick up spareribs at Three Star Barbecue on Joseph Campau in Hamtramck.

On Friday afternoons, Lucy would always laugh and say, "Harry, you shouldn't pick up ribs today. It's not good for the kids." But they both knew it was very good for Jerry and Anne…and very good for them as well. It was a simple time to simply be family.

In the soft stillness of 3 a.m., the four Piaseckis would sit in their small breakfast nook, laugh, tell stories and eat spareribs, French fries, coleslaw, and toasted hamburger buns with garlic butter. Then, once Jerry and Anne went back to bed and fell asleep, Harry would take Lucy in his arms and they would slowly dance in the kitchen to music only they could hear.

"I will love you until the day I die," Harry would whisper.

"Why stop there?" Lucy put her head against his chest to block him from seeing her tears of pure and total love.

"*I'll be loving you...always.*" Harry would softly sing into her hair. "*With a love that's true...always. Not for just an hour...not for just day...not for just a year...but always.*"

# # #

"So that's why I'll always love ribs," Jerry said after telling Rob the whole story. "They really are my childhood,"

The waitress delivered small bowls of coleslaw and retreated quickly toward the kitchen.

"For Anne and me, coming down for 3 a.m. ribs was almost like Christmas morning, maybe even better. I'm not sure exactly what my mom and dad got out of it."

Chapter 3

'Hopelessly Midwestern'. Jerry pulled a CD out of the Jeep's center console. Fortunately, the Jeep was old enough to still have a CD player and Jerry was way too old to know a damn thing about more up-to-date music formats or devices.

He had waited for just the right moment to treat his New Yorker friend to a taste of the Midwest. That moment came the next day as they drove past West Branch, Michigan. (Just a little way up from the crook of the thumb between the pointer and middle fingers if you were identifying the Michigan location on your hand to a friend from an alien environment, like, say, New York for instance.) Jerry always felt that you were truly 'Up North' after you passed West Branch.

Even though Rob could finger pick folk songs on his 12-string guitar with the best of them, and he had intricate knowledge of, as he put it, songs that nobody ever heard of, *'Hopelessly Midwestern'*, wasn't at the top, middle or even bottom of his musical knowledge playlist. Yes, he knew of the song's writer and performer, Joel Mabus, but had never heard what Jerry considered to be a 'Mabus masterpiece'.

"Man you are so unenlightened, uninformed, uneducated, uncultivated, and uninitiated," Jerry tried to sound like Joel Mabus doing the talking blues in the song, but instead, sounded a bit drunk and, perhaps, substantially deranged.

Rob grabbed the CD from Jerry and shoved in into its proper slot on the dashboard. "Let's just listen, what do you think?"

"Unintellectual, unlearned, uncultured, un…"

"I wish I were unconscious," Rob said as Joel Mabus's voice filled the Jeep.

"If you live life in the middle and not on the edge
You're hopelessly Midwestern

If a big Saturday means clipping the hedge
You're hopelessly Midwestern
If you shop at Sears, drink a lot of iced tea
You like to dance the polka and watch TV
Well the jury is in and the critics agree
You're hopelessly Midwestern."

Jerry joined in on the chorus with full and fetid voice.

"Hopelessly Midwestern – corn fed boys and girls
Hopelessly Midwestern – square pegs in this big round
world
  Well, you can go from seas to shining sea
  But right in the middle is the place to be
  And if you like it like that, you're a lot like me –
  Hopelessly Midwestern."

"I think you're just hopeless," Rob laughed.
"Listen and learn Bronx grasshopper," Jerry said while Joel
talked.

"Now if your favorite stretch of highway is flat & straight.
  You're hopelessly Midwestern.
  And you still think sushi looks a lot like bait.
  You're hopelessly Midwestern."

By the time the song finished, Rob was singing along on the
chorus and even trying to anticipate the lyrics in the verses.

"Now, if Carl Sandburg is your kind of poet."

Rob and Jerry belted out: *"You're hopelessly Midwestern!"*

"And if you have an accent but you don't know it!"

"You're Hopelessly Midwestern!"

"Hopelessly, impossibly, irreparably Midwestern."

Rob made Jerry play the song twice more so that he could memorize the guitar chords and play it later. "Got to say it is a good song."

"Damn straight!" Jerry the Michiganian spoke with pride while struggling with the internal quandary many from the state deal with since birth. *Or is it Michigander?*

Jerry moved to play the song for a fourth time, but Rob stopped him. "I think this New Yorker got the message."

New Yorker? Jerry thought. *Or could it be New Yorkiganian?* He brushed away the possibility when he saw an approaching semi carrying Vernors ginger ale.

Jerry stuck his arm out the Jeep's window and pumped his fist up and down at the semi. The driver dutifully responded by honking his air horn twice, his smile growing with each blast.

"My people!" Jerry shouted.

"Jer," Rob said. "Let your people go."

The time passed quickly for Jerry; not so much for Rob.

"And then there's the 500 pound man-killing clam in Cheboygan," Jerry virtually chirped out another childhood memory. If Rob thought, or hoped, for even a single desperate moment that his magical Midwestern mystery tour would have ended with the song, he was woefully incorrect. Jerry was on a roll. He pointed to the top of his index finger to indicate the clam's current location.

"I got a New York finger to share with you."

"That's Mackinaw!" Jerry laughed. "Now about the Mystery Spot in St. Ignace…"

# # #

When they went to Petoskey as children, Anne and Jerry would argue incessantly almost from the moment they got into the car on Packard about whether to see the 'Clam' or the 'Spot' first. By the time they reached Woodward Avenue and turned right for the long drive north, either Lucy, Harry, or both would say: "Do you want us to turn this car around? We will, you know, if you keep fighting."

"You could go to summer school instead of Petoskey," Lucy would pull out the big guns in an effort to establish peace.

This would generally quiet the 'kids' for at least five or ten miles until Anne would poke Jerry's side of the divided seat with her finger, which naturally forced Jerry to retaliate with a pinch. Clearly, he had no choice and every right to avenge his sister's blatant incursion into his sovereign-seat-state.

"She's on my side!"

"He pinched me!"

"Did not!"

"Did too!"

"Not, not, not!"

"Too, too, too!"

Harry and Lucy would sigh, offer road toys, play license plates, sing songs, and do just about anything to help them get through the ride with some semblance of parental sanity still intact. This was before the northern part of Interstate 75 opened from southern Michigan to Mackinaw. Which meant, in the beginning, Harry would drive by, over, or through every small town, stop light, tourist-trap attraction, and train track from the bottom end of the state to the top.

It was as they crossed train tracks that Harry and Lucy would always share a quick glance and squeeze each other's hand. If the train gates were down, they would quickly kiss until either Anne, Jerry or both made gagging noises and accused their parents of sharing 'cooties'.

"Yuck!"

"Ick!"

Both kids secretly loved it when their parents kissed, but they took the childhood obligation of being grossed out by any physical contact between their parents quite seriously, as every serious child should.

# # #

October 28, 1942.

Each morning, Harry would look out of the factory window where he worked near the intersection of Caniff and Oakland on the Hamtramck/Detroit border. He would watch the road until a familiar bus would go bouncing by over the railroad tracks. He would always whisper, "I love you, my darling," kiss the inside of his fingers and press his palm against the glass.

Lucy rode that same bus each and every day without fail. She was 20 years old and a junior at Wayne State University's College of Education near downtown Detroit.

No one in her or Harry's family had ever gone to college. Harry was the first to graduate from high school in his family. Lucy would become the first to graduate from a university. She wanted to teach elementary school students. Harry was so proud of her.

Lucy hated that damn bus. Every morning, she would be sure to be at the stop on time in order to push onto a coach already jammed tight with almost 50 other people going to work, or school, at the start of each day. The bus only had seating for 30, and she knew she would have a half-hour stand in front of her while being squished and jostled every which way as the bus hit pot holes, bumps, and most violently, the railroad tracks at Caniff and Oakland. The only thing that made her smile was the thought of Harry blowing her a kiss as the bus rumbled roughly over the tracks.

On October 28, 1942, Harry watched the bus approach. He kissed his fingers and put his hand against the window. The bus stopped for a north bound freight train. After it passed, even though the warning lights still flashed, several cars drove across the tracks.

The bus driver couldn't see to his right because crammed-in and crunched-up standing passengers blocked his view. He looked at his watch and saw that he was already behind schedule, and would be in line for another balling out—at the very least. The last thing he could do was risk losing his job.

Another car crossed over. *To hell with it*, he thought while putting the bus in gear and stepping on the gas pedal. The bus lurched forward onto the tracks; directly into the path of a speeding southbound passenger train carrying travelers heading to Chicago.

Detroit Free Press – October 1942 –
"Jammed Vehicle Torn in Half; Locomotive Strews Bodies and Wreckage Half a Mile."

**DETROIT AP – Ironwood Daily Globe Michigan –
1942-10-28**
*"Sixteen persons, including at least half a dozen women
and 'some school children' were killed today and more
than a score was injured in a collision of a Detroit Street
Railways bus and a Grand Trunk passenger train...some of
them (the victims) were so badly mangled that a definite
count and positive identification was difficult..."*

DETROIT – (AP) – *"...Bodies were strewn along the
tracks for two blocks, and some were mangled against the
front of the locomotive of the train...The front end of the
bus cleared the tracks, but the locomotive smashed through
the vehicle at its middle doors, cutting it in
half...Schoolbooks of the younger passengers on the bus
were scattered along the right of way. Many of the bodies,
some decapitated and others with limbs severed, were
impossible to identify immediately."*

"Oh my God, no!" Harry could barely get out the words as he
watched the bus Lucy always rode cut in two by the passenger
train. He felt as if his very soul was being torn apart by the
splintering metal and horrendous screams that seemed to come
from inside his being as well as outside the factory.

# # #

Earlier that morning, Lucy was just about to race out the
door to catch the bus when she heard what sounded like a baby
crying from her parents' bedroom. Her father had already
opened the store and her mom had taken him a cup of coffee
and a jelly donut for breakfast.

Ignoring what she assumed was either her imagination or
leaking pipes, Lucy moved toward the front door. She didn't
want to even risk missing the bus. With each step she took, the
crying sound got louder, much louder.

Lucy stopped. "What in the world is that?" She put down
her book bag and walked quickly toward her parents' room just
down a short hallway from the kitchen. As she approached, the
sound of a baby crying seemed to turn into a sob, a softer sound

than a full cry, weaker somehow, but definitely there. Lucy could swear she was hearing it clear as day.

"Mom? Are you back? Who's crying?" When she pushed open the bedroom door, the sobbing sound disappeared. Lucy looked around the bedroom, from the bed to the dresser to the carved rosewood rocking chair with its worn brown leather upholstered seat that her mother had brought with her all the way from Poland. The chair in which Lucy's mom had so often rocked her to sleep as a young child seemed to rock slightly forward and stop. All was silent, all was still.

Lucy didn't have time to wonder about why she imagined that she heard a baby crying. She ran full speed back down the hallway and out the door. "I'm going to miss the damn bus!"

# # #

Harry and his fellow workers raced from the factory and into a nightmare. The bus had burst open when hit by the train. Everyone in the front of the bus was badly injured, except for the driver who was scratched and shaken but relatively unscathed. The passengers in the center and back of the bus had been slaughtered.

Twisted metal, broken glass, and bodies littered the track bed. Some were whole, most were not. The smell and mist of blood filled the air.

Police arriving at the scene tried to hold Harry back, but he shoved one officer aside. "My sweetheart, my Lucy is in there."

For one of the very few times in his life, Harry was openly crying. He wasn't even aware of the tears streaming down his face. "She was on that bus!"

The officers looked at each other and let him pass.

Harry ran among the injured and the dead. He kept shouting his beloved's name. Pieces of human beings were everywhere. Harry picked up a woman's head and gently put it back down in place after seeing that it was someone else's darling.

"Lucy! Lucy! Lucy!"

# # #

Not 20 minutes earlier, Lucy had screamed at the bus as it pulled away from her stop. "Wait! Wait!" She ran as fast as she could while holding on to her book bag and purse. "Stop! Stop the bus!"

The bus didn't stop.

"Damn it!"

Lucy had never missed her bus; that is until the morning of October 28, 1942.

# # #

Harry had never seen such a vision of hell: so many bodies, so much blood. He didn't find Lucy among the survivors. Now he had to search among the dead. He looked at their faces, some with frozen expressions of terror, others with blank empty stares or gently closed eyes. Harry picked up arms, looking at fingers, terrified that he would see the engagement ring he had given Lucy two days earlier. He lifted legs off the ground in search of Lucy's shoes.

# # #

For the first time in her life, Lucy decided to skip school. She would miss two of her four classes anyway, even if the next bus was on time. After relaxing for a bit in the morning sunshine on the bus stop bench, she decided to go back home and get her older brother Ray to drive her to her friend Wanda's house. From there, they could go to Sweetland on Joseph Campau for strawberry sundaes with whipped cream, nuts, and a cherry.

May as well make the best of it, Lucy thought.

Ray and Lucy's parents had given their eldest son money for college tuition several years back and he immediately used it to buy a 1932 Edsel Ford Speedster, which he happily drove to California. Following that adventure, Ray was only allowed back into the house if he agreed to become a carpenter and pay back the money.

As Lucy turned up the walkway to her home, the door flew open and Ray came running out. He leapt down the porch's three front steps and sprinted to his sister, "You're alive. Jesus fucking Christ, you're alive!"

"Ray," Lucy laughed. "Watch your language? Of course I'm alive. Why shouldn't I be? "

"We all thought you were killed."

"For missing the bus?"

"You missed the bus," Ray let out a deep breath. "You missed the bus! That's what saved your life!"

"Ray," Lucy spoke very slowly. "What in the world are you talking about?"

"Frecks just called," Ray couldn't stop the involuntary shaking in his hands. "He said the bus was hit by a train. We all thought you were on it."

Freckles (Dennis) Bobowski was a Detroit cop and good friend of Ray and his brother Walt. He knew their sister Lucy always took that particular bus to Wayne State.

"What about Mom?" Lucy looked toward the house.

"Mom," Ray shouted so loud that the whole neighborhood could hear. "It's Lucy! She missed the goddamn bus!"

Lucy's mom, Felicia Buraczynski, ran out onto the porch. Making the sign of the cross three times, she sat down on the old wooden rocker by the door and prayed.

"Jesus," Lucy felt the blood draining from her face. "I missed the goddamn bus."

"That's probably why you're still breathing," Ray now whispered. "Frecks said a lot of people died. A lot more are torn up pretty bad."

"Oh my God," Lucy suddenly remembered that the only train tracks the bus crossed were the ones that ran north-south next to the factory where Harry worked. She knew that he would have seen the crash as he put his hand against the window just like he did every morning.

Grabbing Ray's arm, Lucy pulled him toward the Speedster which was parked two houses down on the right. "Hurry, Ray! We have to find Harry!"

37

#

Harry sat on track rails still sticky with blood. He hadn't found Lucy, but so many of the bodies were broken beyond recognition. Any one of them could have been his love. He put his head in his stained hands and wept.

"Harry!"

Harry shook his head. He was imagining that he heard Lucy's voice call his name one last time. It sounded like the voice of an angel.

"Harry!" The angel's voice was getting louder, and closer. "Harry! Harry! Harry!"

Leaping to his feet, Harry saw his Lucy running toward him down the tracks. He had to wipe away tears before he fully believed that he was seeing a true miracle unfold. In a moment, he was hugging her as if holding on to dear life.

Chapter 4

So, so, so many decades after the tragic crash, Lucy could still feel Harry's arms around her as he lifted her off the bloody train tracks.

"I thought I lost you. I thought I lost you. My Lucy, my Lucy, my Lucy."

The words Harry whispered that dreadful day were still fresh in her mind. She had grown old without Harry, but in her heart, they both remained forever young and forever in love. For over 35 years, she had remained true to her one true love. She missed him almost every minute of each and every day. His name was the first thing she said each morning, and his face was what she imagined before drifting off to sleep each night. She would talk to his photographs, mostly in loving softness, but occasionally in brittle tones of anger over him dying and leaving her alone. She felt guilty about the anger, "I know you didn't want to die," she would say out loud. "But you did."

Each night she kissed his pillow, which she had kept for all these years. "I love you, Harry, goodnight sweetheart."

Lucy couldn't sleep the night Jerry and Rob spent in Farmington Hills, Michigan. The thought of her son going to Petoskey the next day made her shiver with both trepidation and joy. She moved slowly with her walker around her apartment, occasionally, breaking off a chunk of one of the Hershey chocolate bars with almonds that her son always brought her as a treat. She played solitaire and flipped channels on the television. One of the classic movie stations was playing the original 'The Thin Man'.

Lucy shuddered, closed her eyes, and gripped the arms of the recliner that Harry would have loved. Suddenly, the soft cushioned cloth became the hard leather of the armrests between the seats of Lasky's Movie Theater, and the night turned into the afternoon of December 7th, 1941.

# # #

"Let's go see the new Thin Man movie," Harry said as he walked Lucy home from church that beautiful Sunday morning. "I hear it's just as funny as the first one."

The teenaged couple had seen all three of the earlier Thin Man movies, each starring William Powell and Myrna Loy as Nick and Nora Charles, an ultra-sophisticated, wisecracking couple who solved crimes with a martini in one hand and a dog leash holding their wirehaired fox terrier Asta in the other.

The original *'The Thin Man'* opened in 1934, followed by *'After the Thin Man'* in 1936 and *'Another Thin Man'* in 1939. *'The Shadow of the Thin Man'* opened in movie theaters two weeks before the Japanese attack on Pearl Harbor.

"We can catch the matinee and still be on time for dinner with your folks."

Sunday dinner was a tradition in the Buraczynski household. A chicken would always make the ultimate sacrifice for the event. Attendance was mandatory.

"I'll have to ask my mom if she needs help," Lucy said. "But I think it sounds great."

Lucy's 'help' was not always helpful in the kitchen. So, with Mama Buraczynski's blessing, the couple got to the theater in time for that month's March of Time newsreel titled 'Main Street USA' and a Tom and Jerry cartoon called 'The Midnight Snack'. The movie was scheduled to start at 1:30, but didn't finally get going until almost 2:00.

Lucy often thought of that half hour as being the last 30 minutes of innocence for America as she knew it.

Shortly after 2:30, the film stopped. "Anyone here in the service?" a man's voice shouted from the back of the theater. "You've been ordered to report for duty."

No one in the theater moved for a moment.

"Now!"

Several men in front of Harry and Lucy got up from their seats and quickly walked past them up the aisle. Three other men in uniform immediately left from the row directly behind them.

"What in the world is going on?" Lucy whispered.

Before Harry could say anything the film started up again, but now no one in the audience was paying much attention to the plot. Another ten minutes passed before the film again stopped. This time the house lights came on and a man walked onto the stage in front of the screen.

"Ladies and gentlemen, sorry to tell you this, but the Japs are attacking Pearl Harbor. It's all over the radio. They say it's really bad folks. We're at war."

Lucy squeezed Harry's hand as if she never intended to let go.

At 12:30 in the afternoon the next day, Harry, his brothers and sisters, and their parents gathered around the radio in their living room, as did Lucy and her family in their kitchen. The streets of America fell silent as President Franklin Delano Roosevelt spoke.

"Yesterday, December 7, 1941—a date which will live in infamy—the United States of America was suddenly and deliberately attacked by naval and air forces of the Empire of Japan."

"Now the whole world's gone to shit," Harry's brother Reds said. "Goddamn Japs."

"Shut up, Reds," Harry snapped. "I'm listening."

"Fuck you," Reds said, but stopped talking.

"...the attack yesterday on the Hawaiian Islands has caused severe damage to American naval and military forces. I regret to tell you that very many American lives have been lost."

"Oh my God," Lucy said. "Oh my God."

Lucy's mother and father sat and listened in silence. They had seen war before.

41

"Yesterday, the Japanese Government also launched an attack against Malaya. Last night, Japanese forces attacked Hong Kong. Last night, Japanese forces attacked Guam. Last night, Japanese forces attacked the Philippine Islands.

Last night, the Japanese attacked Wake Island. And this morning, the Japanese attacked Midway Island."

"Busy sons of bitches," Lucy's brother Ray joked without a hint of humor.

"Japan has, therefore, undertaken a surprise offensive extending throughout the Pacific area. The facts of yesterday and today speak for themselves."

Harry's brother, Shy, stared up at the sky from the family's living room window.

"You think the fucking Japs are going to bomb Hamtramck?" Reds snarled or giggled; with him, it was always kind of hard to tell which was which.

Harry, Shy, his four sisters, and his parents all said in union: "Shut up!"

"...hostilities exist. There is no blinking at the fact that our people, our territory, and our interests are in grave danger. With confidence in our armed forces, and the unbounding determination of our people, we will gain the inevitable triumph, so help us God. I ask that the Congress declare that since the unprovoked and dastardly attack by Japan on Sunday, December 7, 1941, a state of war has existed between the United States and the Japanese Empire."

Lucy started to cry.

Harry said, "I have to go see Lucy."

# # #

Thirty-three minutes after the President's speech, the Senate voted 82 to 0 and the House of Representatives 388 to 1 in favor of a declaration of war. The only no vote came from the first woman ever elected to congress, Representative

Jeanette Rankin of Montana who said, "I can't go to war, and I refuse to send anyone else."

After the vote, an angry mob forced her to barricade herself in a telephone booth until Capital Police could escort her to safety.

# # #

Harry and Lucy sat on the Buraczynski's front porch talking of the terrors that awaited them, the country and the world.

"You have to promise me that you won't volunteer. Harry, you have to promise me that, darling."

"But, Lucy, everyone's gotta go."

"And you're gonna go. As you said, everyone has gotta go, but you don't have to be the first. You have an important job at the plant that will help with the war effort. Just keep doing that until they call you up, which you know they will, honey. You'll get your chance, but stay with me for as long as you can."

Harry looked straight forward. He nodded his head just enough to be noticed as an answer to Lucy's plea.

"Do you promise?"

Without turning his head, Harry said, "You know I would promise you anything and always keep that promise."

"Then please say it, Harry."

Harry turned and looked deeply into his Lucy's eyes, "I promise."

Harry had planned to enlist the next day. He changed his plan and kept his promise.

"Here," Harry said, pulling a brand new 1941 Silver Certificate dollar bill from his wallet and quickly tearing it in two. He handed Lucy the larger half.

"What's this for, Harry?"

"It's so that whatever happens, whenever I do get called up, we'll each have half of this dollar to remind us that apart we're only a couple of pieces of torn paper, but together we mean something, something pretty special and pretty forever."

Harry and Lucy held each other all afternoon and well after the sun set in the west.

At 5 o'clock in the morning, Lucy still sat at the small wooden table under the window sill in the living room/dining area of her assisted living apartment. She watched the darkness of the night slowly begin to dissolve into the quiet tenderness of dawn.

Lucy looked at the photo of Harry in his Army Air Corps uniform that she had placed on the table in front of her an hour earlier. In the black and white snapshot, Harry wore sergeant's stripes on his sleeves. She never knew what rank Harry would be in the next photo he would send her from the army. He would be a sergeant in one, a private in the next, a sergeant again, and then back to private. It all depended on whether or not someone succeeded in baiting him into a fight by saying something Harry viewed as crude, cheap, or vulgar about his soon to be wife, Lucy.

It all became a game to his fellow airmen who loved to razz him mercilessly in order to raise his anger and cost him his stripes. The whole squadron would bet on how long it would take for him to be busted back to private. They called it the Crazy Polack Pool, with those selecting the earliest date for demotion generally being the winners.

In the photo before her, Harry was down on one knee in front of his barracks. He wore his full Army Air Corps field uniform complete with freshly shined boots covered by canvas spats laced half way up his shins. His wide brim hat was tipped just a hair toward his right ear. His dress was all regulation, except for the knit gloves he wore on his hands; the gloves Lucy had saved up for and sent him a month earlier. He smiled broadly in the shadow of the hat's brim.

Lucy picked up the photo and stared directly into the eyes of the only man she ever loved. She remembered the 3 am conversation they had that summer Up North so many years ago. *Jerry is going to Petoskey*, she thought before whispering out loud, "Jerry's coming, Harry. He's coming today."

# # #

"Okay, man, just over this hill. Get ready," Jerry's voice was full of excitement and expectation about cresting the hill and seeing the sparkling waters of Little Traverse Bay. "I know this is the hill."

"Yeahhhhhh, rrrrrrright," Rob yawned. Jerry had made the same prediction on the last four hills, but the only thing Rob saw when they reached the top was another hill. This time, however, Jerry was right.

"Wow," Rob stopped his second yawn half-way through. "Wow!"

"It looks the same," Jerry said as the turquoise blue water perfectly reflected the majesty of the sky. The bay was smooth as silk, without ripple or wave. To Jerry, it seemed as though it was welcoming him back to a place where the past became present, the present—the future, and the future once again the past.

"Jer, brake! Brake!" Rob shouted just loud enough to jiggle Jerry away from his mental meanderings in time to avoid running up the back of a slow moving Cadillac with Illinois plates. He slammed on the brakes and fishtailed to the right, finally coming to a stop on the side of the road.

After a minute or so to let the adrenalin that had flooded through his body approach normal levels, Jerry smiled and looked at his pale-faced friend. "So, Rob," he said casually, as if the near wreck experience was nothing out of the ordinary. "Cool, huh?"

"Yeah," Rob's voice stopped quivering as he spoke. "It would be even cooler if we get there alive."

"Don't sweat the small stuff." Jerry pulled the car back onto the road. "I mean, the hospital's right at the bottom of the hill."

The hospital was about the only thing Jerry recognized when they reached the intersection of 131 and 31.

"Didn't we just pass the Apple Tree?" Rob asked, straining back to see the yellow and white four story inn that would be home for the next week.

"Quick drive through town, okay?"

Rob tightened his seat belt, exhaled deeply, and reluctantly agreed, "Sure."

Before the light turned green, Jerry pointed to his left, "That's where my aunt Clara built and ran the first 'motel' in Petoskey back in the early '50s."

The Bay View Inn and Perry Hotel were built much earlier (1886 and 1889 respectively), but Aunt Clara's Petoskey Motor Court was the first 'motel'. Jerry remembered asking as a child what the difference was between a 'ho' and a 'mo'. It had something to do with you being able to park your car right in front of your room in a 'mo', while a 'ho' only had room access from inside corridors.

Of course this had led to a big and heated argument between the grown-ups about the differences between 'mo' and 'ho', at which time Jerry had gone fishing in the Bear River with his cousin Billy.

Jerry shook his head and exhaled slowly as the red light seemed to last forever. The long wait gave him time to see that Aunt Clara's motel was now a Walgreens Pharmacy while Aunt Mary's cabins and Ciocia Babcia's little strip motel across the street were replaced by a Wendy's and a parking lot.

"What the hell is a Ciocia Babcia?" Rob asked.

"You really want to know?"

"No."

When the light finally turned green, Jerry stepped softly on the gas and drove slowly into the past.

The hospital on the left had ballooned in size and was now officially named McLaren Northern Michigan Hospital. But to Jerry, it was still, and would always be, just Northern Michigan Hospital.

The small bakery across the street looked about the same as it did when Jerry and his mom would stop in for glazed donuts and cookies with chocolate sprinkles. Back in the 1950s and '60s, several small motels were built after Aunt Clara paved the way. All of those were gone as well, but the street still looked the same to Jerry as he drove down and over the bridge that spanned the Bear River.

"Maybe we should head to the hotel and check in?" Rob yawned.

"Just ten more minutes," Jerry said as he took a right at the fork in the road and drove up Mitchell Street past rows of stores, many of which like the tiny JCPenney store on the corner of Mitchell and Howard streets and the Mitchell Street Pub remained in place. They looked just as Jerry remembered them from his childhood when he ran down the street in red clam diggers and dirty white high top sneakers. To his continuing embarrassment, Jerry recalled his mom dragging him into Penney's for back-to-school clothes and calling out for all to hear: "Where do you have husky sizes?"

Neither Jerry nor Anne had been allowed into the Mitchell Street Pub when they were kids, as it was best known as the place where Ernest Hemingway is said to have practiced drinking as a young man.

Jerry slowed the car to take in the memories before heading past the relatively new library and up the hill to the house with a 20-foot porch and hanging bench swing that he and Anne had enjoyed on many a warm Petoskey summer afternoon.

Jerry pulled into a church parking lot next door in order to turn around and head back down the street. Once again over the Bear River, he made a right turn and drove down to the long breakwater where he had fished as a kid. After being damaged in a storm, the breakwater, which protected docks nestling luxury cabin cruisers and sail boats, was rebuilt with a wider walking area to make it 'safer for families to enjoy'.

"They fucking neutered it," Jerry said before starting to turn the car around in the new parking area for tourists. Taking a backward glance into the rearview mirror, Jerry suddenly slammed on the breaks and put the car in reverse. There, at the end of the breakwater, he saw a man wearing a baseball cap and fishing waders. "Look at that fisherman out there," he said, pointed and looked at Rob. "I know that guy."

"You know what guy?"

"The fisherman, I swear he's the same guy that…"

Jerry stopped mid-sentence. The only people on the breakwater were a young couple carrying a small child and a middle-aged business man on a cell phone.

"Ahh-huh," Rob patted his friend on the shoulder. "I think you need a rest."

I know he was there, Jerry thought.

It looked like the same guy Jerry had seen fishing on the river and the breakwater before; many, many years before. *Just my imagination. Not possible. Just not possible.*

In his mind, Jerry heard his mother's whisper, *"You never know about Petoskey."*

# # #

Lucy hugged Harry's army photo to her chest, which she tended to do every morning, at least once during the day and then when she said; "Good night, sweetheart. Love you always." She would softly kiss the photo. "Forever."

Memories and moments together flooded her being and seemed to swirl through the air around her in a soft and loving frenzy of joy and laughter—sadness and sorrow.

She smiled when she remembered the first real meal she ever made for her husband. After the war when Harry had returned from the South Pacific, Lucy had joined him in off-base living quarters available to married troops in Pratt, Kansas. For some reason, she chose to start her cooking career with galumpkis (Polish stuffed cabbage). A steak dinner would have been a piece of cake, Spaghetti—as easy as pie; Galumpkis, on the other hand, pose as much risk as they promise reward.

Lucy's mom had written down the recipe and procedures involved in becoming a master galumpki-maker. She included 27 ingredients and 33 separate steps from boiling the cabbage leaves, to the meat filling, to the rolling, to the sauce. She wrote it all in Polish so that she knew there would be no mistake. "Just follow what I wrote exactly, and they will be delicious." Her mom wanted to give her daughter courage and support, although she secretly wished Lucy had decided to start with kielbasa and boiled potatoes.

Lucy gathered the ingredients together and did exactly what was written. Harry loved her mother's galumpkis, and she wanted to surprise him with a special meal when he came home from the base. And, surprise him she did.

By following the directions to the letter, the novice cook had no idea that her mom had accidentally left out a few of them, specifically those 'letters' that spelled out the word 'cooked' before the word 'rice'.

Oh, Lucy carefully measured the amount of rice to be used. "Exactly two cups," she said to herself as she poured the rice from a bag into a large measuring cup. Nodding her head, she dumped it right into the meat. In the end, the result was what could only be described as 'crunchy galumpkis', upon one of which Harry had lost a filling.

"I don't know what I did wrong," Lucy actually started to cry at the table.

Harry reached across and took both of her hands in his. "They are delicious." He ate three more at that sitting and two more before they went to bed.

For the rest of his life, Harry would often speak of the best galumpkis he ever had. "They were out of this world!"

That first week Lucy also followed Harry's sister Mary's babka recipe. Harry didn't have an opportunity to tell loving lies because the babka couldn't be cut by a knife, and a handsaw was somehow unseemly. This time they both laughed.

"But Mary's babka always comes out perfect," Lucy picked up the loaf and dropped it back on the table with a thunk.

"Yeah," Harry agreed. "Remember, honey, my sister likes being the one and only Babka Queen."

"True. So?"

"So do you think she would tell you everything she puts in it?"

"Or maybe she told me to add some ingredients that she doesn't."

"Like concrete?"

"Like concrete."

They used the babka as a door stopper for a few days before throwing it out in the backyard for the birds. The birds passed on the offer and the babka stayed in place until they moved out of the house when Harry was discharged from the army in 1946.

# # #

Lucy held the photo out in front of her, "Maybe that darn babka is still there. What do you think, Harry?" she said softly to the young man in uniform that she loved so dearly from that day in the candy store to this in assisted living. Lucy again embraced the photo, closed her eyes, and drifted.

"Down by the O-Hi-O."

In her heart, Lucy could hear Harry joyously belting out a song as he hammered his fingers down on a ukulele he brought home from the army.

"I've got the cutest little oh my oh."

Harry didn't know how to play the ukulele but could sing in his own unique key on command.

"There ain't nobody half as pretty as she... And sweet as can be... And jumpin' jeepers creepers she's crazy for me... And what an oh my oh..."

Whatever song Harry sang, he would strum the strings with the same ferocious vigor and let his voice carry the tune. He loved singing everything from *'I'm a Ding Dong Daddy from Dumas,'* to *'Don't Sit Under the Apple Tree'* and *'Ain't She Sweet'.*

When Lucy mentioned one day that she happened to be 5 foot 2 inches tall, well, Harry went wild in voice and on the uke.

"Five foot two...eyes of blue...but oh what those five foot could do...has anybody seen my gal..."

"Harry, my eyes are brown."

"Five foot two...eyes of brown...let's go out and paint the town...has anybody seen my gal..."

Then he personalized it with—*"Five foot two...eyes of brown...Lucy never lets me down...has anybody seen my gal..."*

This went on for a week before Lucy threatened to bake another babka if he continued.

Harry, eventually, put away the ukulele but never stopped singing. If anyone's voice could travel through time, it would be Harry's. Lucy thought of the Christmas Eve when he came prancing through the front door singing *'Deck the Halls'* at the top of his lungs.

"DECK THE HALLS WITH BOWS OF HOLLY...FA LA LA LA LA..."

On the 'FA LA LAs' the Christmas tree that Lucy and the kids had just finished putting up came crashing down, shattering dozens of ornaments against the large round black lacquered coffee table that stood nearby.

With a shocked expression Harry started whisper-singing; *'Silent Night'*.

Despite the mess, even Lucy had to laugh. Harry could always make her laugh. It would often only take a certain look, a wink, a glance, a crooked smile to make Lucy giggle and bubble over with love.

Then again, there were other moments that were far less subtle. Lucy thought of Harry lighting firecrackers in the backyard with Jerry. On one particular Fourth of July, she and her husband had set up a brand new aluminum swimming pool on the driveway. It stood about 18 inches high and perhaps 10, maybe 12 feet around. Having filled it to the point of almost overflowing, Harry wanted to show his son how you could throw a cherry bomb into the water and it would still explode.

Lucy had watched from the kitchen window as her husband lit the round red firecracker's green wick with his cigarette and tossed it toward the pool. His aim was just slightly off. Instead of going into the water, the cherry bomb landed on the cement and rolled up flat against the aluminum. She would always remember Harry's expression in the few seconds that followed as the fuse burned. His eyes widened, and his jaw dropped. The cherry bomb exploded with such force that the metal blew open and a tidal wave of water flooded down the driveway.

Lucy laughed so hard that Anne came running down from upstairs. "What happened, Mom?"

Lucy could barely get out the words, "Daddy blew up the swimming pool."

They both looked out the window. Harry just stood there with his hands on his hips staring at the tiny pieces of aluminum floating by and wondering how he was going to explain this one to Lucy.

While Harry maintained ownership of the title: Loudest Person Ever by right of having sung down the Christmas tree, Anne would give him a run for his money. The 'Loudness Contests' could erupt anywhere, from the kitchen table to the living room couch, from the car to Aunt Helen's cottage. It would all begin when Harry gave his daughter a special nod and both would screech out, "HAAAAAAAAAAAAAA!" at decibel levels that defied description.

After about five seconds, give or take a tick or two, both Harry and Anne would look at Lucy. "Who won?"

Carefully removing her hands from her ears, Lucy would generally declare the contest a draw, which meant both Anne and her father could walk away confidently proclaiming victory…as loudly as possible.

'Loudness Contests' between Harry and Anne could break out at any time, and often involved lyrics as well as just pure noise. They could happen during the singing of the national anthem before baseball games, whenever old acquaintances should not be forgot, and always at birthday parties where the two would drown out all other Happy Birthday singers and sometimes make a young birthday boy or girl cry or run from the candle-lit cake.

"Oh you two," Lucy would say with mock disgust.

At this point, Harry and Anne would simply look at each other, smile broadly, and either say "Oh well", or begin another round of competition.

Inside, Lucy was smiling too.

So many memories of a life now long lost but always lingering in Lucy's heart and soul. She whispered softly, "I love you" as she gently brought the photo of Harry up to her lips. She thought about how she had tried to be a good mother, and how Harry had been the very good daddy she always knew he would be. Those thoughts took her back to yet another memory; one of the sweetest and then most bitter of her life.

Chapter 5

Harry and Lucy married on Saturday, May 22, 1943. Harry had been inducted into the Army in late November 1942. By March 1943 he was assigned to the United States Army Air Corps where he would train as a gunner and bombardier. He was stationed in Texas at the Big Spring Bombardier School. Harry and Lucy would write every day. That December, Lucy was planning a week-long visit, for which Harry had his own specific plans in mind.

December 15, 1943.

Darling Lucy,

I love you very much dear and miss you more than ever. I just can't wait till you get here, darling. So please hurry. Honey, did you get the reservation because they will be very hard to get over the holidays. But if you are coming by Pullman, I guess it won't be so bad. It won't be a very long trip. It should take you about 25 hours to get here, and I will be waiting at the depot.

It is very cold here, but not for me because I wear my flying suit all the time, and it does keep me nice and hot. I am sure the cold won't bother you because I'm going to keep you very warm. Gee, I love you, darling, more than I can say, honey, and I will prove it to you when you come down here to see me.

Honey, will you try to bring down a pint of whiskey so that we can have a couple of toasts together over the holidays, and we might even get drunk. I want to see you drunk because I have never seen you get drunk yet, and you haven't seen me drunk yet either. But don't bring the pint if you don't want to.

Gee, I love you so much that I can't wait till I can be kissing you again, just like I used to, honey. Won't we have fun, eh? Maybe we can even try to make a child, eh, dear? Do you think it could be possible for us to try?

I love you very, very much…

Your very own hubby,

Harry.

Lucy brought the pint. They tried. They tried a lot. Then the one week visit ended.

January 2, 1944.

Hello Darling Lucy,

Gee, honey, it's only hours since we were in each other's arms and already I miss you so very much. It was very hard for us to part, honey. I just had cramps all over when you left on the train. I tried not to cry in front of you, but honey as the train pulled us apart, I started to cry like a baby.

Gee, honey, I hate this darn army more than ever because it is keeping us apart, but honey I am always at your side wherever you go and whatever you may be doing. I love you honey, and it will take more than this war to keep us apart, our love is stronger and full of life and joy.

Your very own hubby,

Harry.

PS; Maybe soon you will be calling me Daddy, eh honey?

Lucy's response arrived on January 14th, 1944.

Dear Daddy,

My darling, you said that I might be calling you "daddy", soon and you might be right. I have not been to the doctor, I think it's too soon, but it is possible that we really did make our child during my visit. Now don't worry about anything. I really don't know for sure yet. But, I love you so much, and I had to tell you what is happening, or

54

maybe to say it better what is not happening this month, if you know what I mean.

Keep your fingers crossed…Daddy

I love you.
Always yours,
Lucy.

January 14, 1944

Dear Mommy,

I fell off my bunk when I read your letter, and I have a top bunk. Don't worry, I wasn't hurt, just so, so, so happy, darling. It's good none of the fellows were in the barracks, or they would have thought I was sauced up or something. When will you go to a doctor? 'Til then, I am keeping everything I can keep crossed—crossed.

If it's a boy, let's name him Tommy. I always wanted a son named Tommy. Is that okay, sweetheart? Tommy?

I really want to be there when we have our baby, and he will be the best baby in the whole world because he will be ours and only ours. I will try to be a good father and maybe I will succeed if I try very hard. Won't it be grand when that heavenly day comes, dear?

It will be hard for you, darling, but please don't worry because I will make sure that you have the best of everything, and I will be at your side no matter where I will be or what I am doing. Just don't worry about me because my heart and soul will be there to guide you to safety.

…please take care of yourself because without you I have no reason to live.

Your very own hubby,
Daddy Harry.

February 3, 1944.

My Darling,

Honey, why can't you be with me forever? It really isn't fair. I hate this war business just as much as you do. I don't know how I am going to stand much more of this. Oh, honey, it's so miserable here! There's no 'living', just an existence; that's all.

In your letter, you asked me to tell you definitely about the baby. As of yet, I don't know, dear. I guess this might be it. Darling, I am scared without you here. I am terribly scared. I don't know how I will go through with it if it really is so. I want you here with me because it's hard, honey. Please don't think I'm a baby, it's just that this is the first time and I wish my husband were here. I have such an awful feeling in me, dear…such an awful feeling.

I saw your sister, Helen, today. She was to a fortune teller who told her that she would have a baby in 9 months, and I in 8 months. The woman also told Helen that you would go overseas in two months. That means you won't even see the baby and won't be here. Oh, honey, it just can't be so—it can't.

I kinda hinted about the baby to my mother. I didn't tell her—just in a kidding way. She thought I was kidding too. Oh, honey, I wish you could be here to help me break the news if it's true. I don't know how. It's all so complicated and I am so scared.

Goodnight for tonight dearest. I love you very much. Please forgive me if I seemed a bit selfish in this letter… Just feeling kinda down in the dumps today.

Always your own.
Lucy.

P.S. Do you think we might be able to get off-base married housing sometime soon? Then maybe I can have Tommy there, with you.

February 19, 1944

Hello My Dearest Darling Lucy,

I love you very much darling…you're everything to me. My dreams and thoughts are of you darling, and I just love to dream about you, our child, and our future together as a family; you, me, and Tommy…

Darling, about us living near camp as a family, well, nothing is official, and I don't know what will happen to me. So as soon as something develops, I will let you know, OK baby?

I love you darling with all my heart and that's where I will always be your very own Daddy Harry.

Kisses and love forever and forever,
Harry.

Later on February 19th, as the sun set on a crystal clear Texas sky, Harry wrote:

Hello Sweetheart,

Gee I wish this war would be over so that I could come home for good and just not have to worry any more like I do now. I am feeling in tip top shape; nothing wrong with me. I just hate the army, that's all... There are a lot of rumors that we might ship out, but as far as I know, it's just rumors.

...our child will always be proud of his parents because, really darling, we are going to give him all the things that we wanted and could not have while we were kids. I am so sure that he will be a perfect baby with all his mother's features.

Oh, darling, I am so thrilled just to think that I might be a father and can't wait to tell the world all about it. But, for now, let's keep it under our hats until we know Tommy is on the way. This is our secret, our dream.

I love you Mommy—From Daddy
Your very own hubby,
Harry.

The next word Harry got from Lucy on the subject came in the form of a telegram ten days later. She was too excited to write a letter and wait for a response.

Western
Union

Despite the cost, Harry was on the telephone in minutes to tell his Lucy that she had made him the happiest man in the world.

"Let's still keep it our secret, at least for a while, okay baby?"

"Why darling?" Lucy asked.

"Just a gut feeling. I guess I don't want to jinx it."

"Shh, don't even say that."

"Lucy, let's do that, you know, keep it secret for our Tommy; if it's okay with you, sweetheart."

"Okay, whatever you say, darling."

"Promise, Mommy?"

"Promise, Daddy!"

Lucy kept her promise for exactly 37 hours and 10 minutes.

February 29, 1944

Dearest Harry,

Darling, I told mother about the baby today. At first she was kinda peeved, but later, she actually was happy and began planning with me all about what we will get for it. They've already decided that I would move into the bigger bedroom in the summer. They are going to have it redecorated…very baby-like. They're also going to dig a basement because when the baby comes, we're in need of steam heat so that he will always be warm and very well.

Mom said that she will buy the crib and a special dresser for the baby. She insists on doing that. Honestly, Harry, she's really happy and is having so much fun planning, and she can hardly wait until he comes.

I'm very happy too, Darling. I just wish you were here with me, but the war will probably be over soon and then we'll be forever together. We will be so happy. We will build our home, and it will be the most

58

beautiful home—better than any ones we know, and boy will they all be jealous.

Well, dear, I guess that's all for now. I'll close for tonight with all my love.

Goodnight, Sweetheart. 'I'll be loving you always.' Your very, very own,

Lucy.

Knowing that Lucy had spilled the baby-beans, upon finishing her letter Harry raced to the back of the barracks where a bunch of the fellas were shooting craps.

"I'm having a baby!" Harry smiled so broadly that his jaw ached. "Me! A baby! Goddamn! I'm going to be a Goddamn father!"

"Just what we need, another little Harry fucker running around," his best friend Wally laughed.

"Wally," Harry grabbed both of his buddy's shoulders. "I am having a fucking baby!"

Wally looked down at Harry's stomach. "You don't even look a little knocked up."

"Well, I am, we are, I-I-I mean *she* is."

"Oh, you mean Lucy's got a bun in the oven," another buddy, Tony said. He got up and handed Harry the dice. "That's swell, Harry, the bones are yours."

Tony paused for a second before saying, "By the way, who's the fucking father?"

That was the type of joke that usually cost Harry his stripes, but on this day, he just didn't care. He was happier than he had ever been in his life. "I'm feeling lucky," Harry laughed. "I'm feeling like the luckiest man on earth!"

Harry rolled the dice, by the time he was finished, he had won one hundred dollars, which he immediately sent home to Lucy.

March 8, 1944

Darling Harry,
Where in the world did you get so much money? You're not doing anything to get into trouble are you? Remember, Tommy and I are depending on you...
Forever yours with love and kisses,
Lucy.

March 17, 1944

Hello my dearest darling Mommy Lucy,
Don't you worry about me getting thrown into the pokey. I am going to be a Daddy, and I want to be the best one I can be. No one wants a jailbird for a daddy. I want our baby to think a lot of me. I am sure that he will be a perfect baby with all of his mother's features, because I sure don't want him to look like me or worse my ugly cuss brother Reds... I am so thrilled just to think that I might be a father. I told all the fellas. They razzed the hell out of me, but I didn't care... Honest darling, I do a lot of thinking about us here. Our days are ahead of us, and we will make good use of them won't we? You and me and Tommy make three!
Love to Mommy from Daddy, your very own hubby,
Harry.

March 24, 1944

Hello my Harry,
I don't know how much more I can take your not being here, darling. I am scared. I am not really sure why, so far so good as they say. It's just, I don't know, a feeling inside. Any more news about your shipping out? Maybe they will send you to Chicago and that way you'll be so much closer when we have Tommy. Texas is just so darn far away. I don't mean to gripe. I know you would be here if you could be. I just feel kinda blue and missing you. I have a doctor's appointment day after tomorrow. I bet he says that I'm just being a silly goose and it's all perfectly normal for someone having a

first child. I'm just being a jumpy worrywart. I sure don't want you to feel the same.

Yours forever—Love you forever,

Lucy.

Two days later, Lucy left work early. The pain started just before 10 a.m. and became almost unbearable by noon. She had scheduled a doctor visit for 4 p.m. that day, but called him on the phone to cancel. That evening she wrote;

Harry Dear,

I didn't keep my appointment with the doctor today because I was feeling pretty bad at school. I had such awful cramps in my stomach that it was all I could do to get home from work. When I came home, I went straight to bed and stayed there for hours. I'm feeling better after the rest, so I'll try to make it to the doctor tomorrow if he can take me.

I tried calling your sister, Helen, today, but she said she was too busy to talk. She doesn't call anymore, none of them do. They must be ticked off over one thing or another. I have no idea what I did to make them so, but I wonder if they are all jealous about the baby. I know my mom told your mom, so they might be peeved that I didn't tell them myself. Gee, Harry, I am sorry if I did anything wrong. I just didn't want anyone else here to know until I'm further along. Oh well, now they do know so you can probably expect them to tell you off in a letter. Sorry.

Your loving wife always,

Lucy.

March 30, 1944

Hello My Dearest Darling,

Did you see the doctor? What did he say? I'm sorry you were feeling so bad but happy that you are feeling better. This damn war gives everyone the heebie geebies, that's probably what made you sick and blue. I hate the army more than ever now that Tommy is coming, and I want to be with you more than I can ever say. Please just take care of yourself.

I am feeling as well as ever, in the best of health, and in very good condition. I am taking special care of myself. My face is nice and clear, and I weigh 170 pounds. That's not bad at all, is it darling? It's important because I want my mommy to love me when I come back. I don't want to be sloppy. I want to be a lot better physically fit than I was before, and I want our baby to think a lot of me. I shave daily and clean my nails regularly and clean my teeth and brush my hair and keep very fit. I'm doing it all for you, darling, all for you and Tommy.
Your own daddy hubby,
Harry.

PS: *Don't worry about Helen or the rest of them. What we do is nobody else's business. They haven't written about the baby yet. If they do, you know I will just tell them to go to hell.*

April 3, 1944

Darling Harry,

Yes, I did see the doctor. He said everything looked pretty good, but that I need to have a little operation to change the position of the baby. I don't want you to worry about it because it isn't very serious. The doctor says it isn't dangerous at all now; it's just that it has to be done before the baby grows much bigger because if we wait too long it would do harm and would cause terrific back aches because the baby would be in the back. Please don't worry darling because it isn't anything—it's very minor. In fact, I don't have to have it right now, but sometime in the next few weeks. What do you think? Maybe I should do it now and just get it over with.
All my love always,
Lucy

PS: *Don't tell your family to go to hell. That will just make them more peeved than ever.*

Lucy decided to go in for the procedure the next day. Her letter to Harry dated April 3rd, arrived on the 8th; three days after she had called her darling Harry to tell him she had lost the baby.

On the 4th of April Harry had written;

My dearest mommy Lucy,

Honey, please take good care of yourself and our Tommy for me while I am away because I love you both very much. Gee, honey, I wish that we already had the baby because I want one real bad. But, honey, please don't take anything that will harm you and don't go to just any common doctor. Try to get the best. I want you to have the best of everything and don't worry about the money. We will have more than enough. I will see to that, honey.

I love you, darling, and I want you to have the best because even that isn't good enough for you. We are going to have the perfect baby, and he will be just like you. Tommy will have the best mommy, I know that darling, I know that in my heart...

...I've been doing a lot of thinking about our future, darling. Gee I just imagine what a lovely home we will have. We will have it just the way we want it, and we won't take anybody else's advice. Our home will be the bestest of any of them, and we will work on it until we get it perfect.

Your own Hubby Daddy,
Harry.

Lucy called Harry shortly after he got off duty on Wednesday, April 5th, 1944. She was crying when he answered so he didn't even have to ask a question. All Harry said as tears filled his eyes and sorrow engulfed his being was: "I love you so very, very, very much."

After several minutes, Lucy managed to say: "I am so sorry, darling, I lost the baby."

Harry choked on his tears. "I know, darling. I know."

For the next half hour, Harry and Lucy cried together. They prayed for Tommy. After whispering goodnight, they each cried and prayed alone.

April 10, 1944

My Darling Lucy,
   Are you sorry that you married me?...
   Love always,
   Harry.

April 14, 1944,

Harry, my Harry,
   Darling, I'm surprised that you ask that because you know that I'll never regret that. I'm very proud and happy that I'm your wife, and I wouldn't want it any other way. Remember that always. I love you darling and I always will...
   Goodnight sweetheart.
   Ever your own,
   Lucy.

Minutes after sealing that letter, Lucy wrote another:

Harry darling,
   I'm so sorry that you feel so badly about the baby darling, but we did our best. It isn't our fault, dear. Maybe I'm just no good. When we try again, we'll find out for sure because lots of times it takes several tries. Maybe as you said, it's all for the best. Now we'll save money, and when we're a little more comfortably settled, we can start our little family because I'm pretty sure that we're going to have the most precious family in the world.
   Dearest, I am sure that all too soon you will be pushing a carriage and walking the floors at night. You'll sure have some fun with Tommy then, eh?
   Don't worry about me. I'm fine, sad of course, but fine physically and in my heart.
   Your 'for always' loving wife,
   Lucy

April 21, 1944

Darling Lucy,

You are the greatest mommy a daddy can ever have. I was way down in the dumps, but your letters made me understand that we are only at our start and our happy days are just around the corner. I know when we do have our Tommy that he will be the most precious baby ever. He will be that because you'll be his mom. I can only hope and pray that I will be there with you when Tommy is born, and we can start our forever together...
All my love,
Harry.

April 27, 1944

My dearest Hubby,

Today I received your letter where you said our happy days are just around the corner. It made me as happy as I could possibly be. Your letters always make me feel that way because I'm terribly in love with you and miss you more than I can say. Maybe you'll get a furlough soon, or I can come down and stay with you there for a while. Maybe we can start again on our Tommy—what do you think about that?
Honey, it's only for a short while that we're apart again—just think that soon we will be together for good. It's all I'm living for, darling daddy. You are all I want because I belong to you—all of me—and you belong to me.
Your loving wife,
Lucy.

A week later, Harry's unit shipped out for Guam.

In 1945, Harry was one of the members of his squadron who came back to the women they loved. Many others suffered a different fate. Harry and Lucy never did have their 'Tommy' but later, Lucy gave birth to Anne, and then almost four years after Anne, Jerry was born.

# # #

"Did I ever tell you that my dad always wanted a son named Tommy?" Jerry said to Rob as they crossed US 131 and the Walgreen's drug store that replaced Aunt Clara's motel.

"No," Rob said. "How did you end up being a Jer?"

"My grandmother, my mom's mom, knew a Tomek in Poland."

"So?"

"She said he was the village idiot."

"Sounds perfect," Rob joked.

"Asshole," Jerry smiled. "No, my mom said my grandmother kept chanting: 'Tomek Tomek *w dupe dzwonek*.'"

"And what might that mean?"

"Translated it's something like Tommy Tommy has a bell ringing in his ass." Both men laughed.

"She also used to say: '*Maslo dupka trzasla*' or, in proper English, Jerry cleared his throat, butter goes to your butt."

"Now that one makes sense," Rob said. "My grandmother would always send out curses in perfect Yiddish, one of her favorites was '*Vaksn zolstu vi a tsibele mitn kop in dr'erd un dif is farkert*'."

"My turn to ask what might that mean?"

"May you live like an onion with your head in the ground and your feet in the air."

"I think our grannies would get along just fine."

"No doubt about it," Rob said happily. "The Bubbe-Babcia mafia would rule the world. Or at least make it feel guilty as hell."

"There's the Apple Tree." Jerry pointed to the left as they approached the hotel. "Home at last."

As he pulled into the driveway to the Apple Tree Inn, Jerry wondered what it would have been like to be Tommy.

Chapter 6

Jerry loved the Apple Tree Inn. It stands slightly up the hill from where the Petoskey Motor Court once set the standard for comfort and traveler luxury. Back then the neon sign in front of the Motor Court proudly informed all drivers of its 'ultra-modern' nature, while pointing the way to the lobby via a large yellow arrow with sequentially blinking lights.

What was considered 'ultra-modern' in the year 1957 involved a table fan in every room, a 19-inch black and white television set, and a turquoise princess phone by the bed. Orange motel room doors faced a flat neatly mowed courtyard with a single small tree and multiple round metal picnic tables with yellow, blue, and green umbrellas sticking up from the holes in the middle. The bouncy orange metal chairs that accompanied the tables had branded many a tourist's bottom when they sat down on them without thinking on a hot, super-sunny summer afternoon.

Jerry was envisioning countless moments and memories of Petoskey as he followed Rob down the driveway and into the lobby of the Apple Tree. Parking was in the back, so the travelers had a short trek from the Jeep to the hotel office.

Jerry intentionally lagged behind a bit, smelling the northern air and feeling a serenity that New York City could never really offer. It was as if he was meant to be in this exact place at this exact time. The air felt both soft and invigorating, as if welcoming him back, both to the past and the present. He also felt the phrase 'it's about time'.

That's what I get for being a writer, he smiled to himself. *Can't just think: gee, what a nice day,* Jerry chuckled.

He couldn't remember the last time, if there had ever been a last time, that he had used the word 'gee'.

The fairly large guest rooms at the Apple Tree Inn are simple, clean, quite basic, and pretty. The view from every balcony is breathtaking. Over each traditional, white, vertical, plastic railing, one sees the expanse of Petoskey below transition into the majestic blueness of Little Traverse Bay. During the day, sunlight sparkles on still water or dances in golden bursts off ripples or waves. After sunset, the black expanse of water is delicately interrupted by the rhythmic blinking of the light tower, calling boaters and sailors to safe haven in Harbor Springs across the way. The soft green light is a signal to those watching it reflect on the water that everything is as it should be in the night.

After checking in and chatting with the wonderfully friendly clerk and hotel manager, Jerry and Rob headed off toward their rooms: 406 and 410. As they walked, Jerry invited Rob to join him for dinner at the Mitchell Street Pub.

"Thanks, man," Rob smiled. "But I think you and your memories deserve to spend a little 'alone time' together."

"You sure?"

"Yep," Rob said as they reached his room first. Sliding the key card into the slot, he opened the door when the light on the key pad flicked from red to green. "For this boy, it's just pizza, a little CNN, and crash city. That's about all I can handle for the rest of the day and night."

"Okay," Jerry shook his head. "I guess the story of Aunt Mary's meatloaf with whole hard boiled eggs inside can hold till tomorrow."

"Or longer," Rob laughed while stepping into his room.

"It was like big, slimy, yellow eyes were staring up at you from each slice."

As the door closed, Jerry heard Rob call out, "A lot, lot, lot longer."

Once in his room, Jerry halfway unpacked, took a long look at the bay from the balcony, checked his e-mail on his iPad, and headed back to the Jeep. His first stop would be at the Hub Bar on Crooked Lake in Oden, about 10, 12 miles or so up on Route 31 from Petoskey. The last time he had seen the place was well over 20 years earlier when he was visiting his daughter who spent several summers at Camp Algonquin on Burt Lake, which is another nine or ten miles up the road on route 68.

At the fork in the road in downtown Petoskey, Jerry veered left this time instead of right and headed out along the bay past the beautiful and nostalgic Stafford's Bay View Inn, quaint bed and bread and breakfasts, McDonald's and a number of small strip malls complete with grocery stores, pharmacies, and laundromats.

Staying on 31, he passed the turnoff to M 119 that would have taken him to Harbor Springs, with its waters often filled with children learning to sail on tiny sunfish sailboats, and colorfully named cruisers and yachts securely moored to its pristine docks.

Jerry smiled remembering some of the names lettered lovingly on the sterns of the boats. Names like *INDECISION*, *BEATS SMOKING, JOE'S FOLLY,* and Jerry's all-time favorites: *WET DREAM* and *BITE ME*. (The latter appearing on a fishing boat out of Luddington.)

Harry Piasecki had also considered purchasing a bar in Harbor Springs back when the possibility of The Hub was still in play, but it was just too pricey in a community noted for its expansive lakeside mansions and heavily-monied summer people from Chicago and beyond. Besides, Harry was drawn by the roadside presence, belly-up to the bar ambience, and happy slap on the back camaraderie of The Hub.

"The Hub just feels right, don't you think, honey?" Harry asked Lucy in the bar's gravel and grass parking lot on the last day of their full summer in Petoskey. "It's really special here. Do you think so too?"

Lucy had to admit that she did feel comfortable and at peace Up North, and she loved Harry's sense of enthusiasm for the place. But she had been raised and reared to be practical above all else, with the only 'senses' that mattered being either 'common' or 'horse'. While Harry was a dreamer, Lucy's dreams had been limited by training and the times to marriage, a few years of teaching and a lifetime of family management.

In elementary school, her parents would only allow her to wear practical, but clunky, Endicott Johnson shoes that they sold in one corner of the store. She longed for the fancier shoes, those with buckles or bows, that many of the girls wore, but her folks would have none of such silliness.

"You have sensible shoes right here," her mom would dismiss all pleas for patent leather. "In Poland, many girls have no shoes at all."

Later in life, Lucy had, for just a moment or two, fantasized about travel and being a reporter. Instead, her family convinced her that if a *lady* had to work, she would be best served by being a teacher so she could have the summers off to be with her children when they were on a break from school.

"You know," Lucy would smile and say years later. "That was really the right decision. I never regretted it. I wouldn't trade it for the world." She meant the statement with 99% of her heart; on some days, 98%.

So while Harry envisioned making The Hub home, Lucy thought only of the nest she had built for her family almost 300 miles to the south. Harry knew the sacrifices she had made to be with him, and the sacrifices he would make to be with her.

On that day in the parking lot, when Lucy hadn't responded immediately to his questions, he didn't press for an answer. Instead, he just kissed her on the head and said: "Maybe someday, baby. Just you and me. Maybe someday."

"Maybe someday," Lucy had snuggled close, happy to be off the hook but also somehow knowing somewhere deep inside that what Harry had said was true.

Jerry drove past a miniature golf course with a pirate ship, a series of restaurants, and finally open northern Michigan land— filled with beauty, waterways, and wonder. Passing the two railway cars, one turquoise and one a deep, dull red sitting on the left side of the road that Jerry remembered from childhood, he knew he was very close to The Hub.

Still one mile turned to two, three, and five. "Where the hell is The Hub?" he said as he kept his eyes peeled to the right hand side of the road where, as expected, he saw Crooked Lake, but not the white house with the words *'The Hub – Famous For Food'* written on the side under the peaked, dull, rust-colored roof. The place held such significance to his childhood; 'both' of which now appeared to be long gone.

"Damn."

The waters of the lake gave way to trees and land on his right. He knew he had gone too far when he spotted the Oden State Fish Hatchery on his left. Still, Jerry smiled. The Hatchery was always a point of interest for the Piaseckis when Anne and Jerry were little. It held particular allure for Jerry and his dad. The hatchery stood between The Hub and the right turn to Pellston, which is where everyone would take a left turn toward Mackinaw.

"Wow," Jerry said as he quickly turned into the fish hatchery which had clearly done a great deal of 'hatching' of its own over the previous decades. He remembered driving to the hatchery with his family, somehow also recalling a white knitted T-shirt with a yellow sailboat on the front that his father wore from time to time. He laughed as his mind wandered to the most vivid recollection of that T-shirt, which was of it being upside down as his dad slipped and plunged head first into the St. Clair river while launching a row boat for one of their fishing adventures.

He came up from the water about 20 feet down current, embarrassed a bit, and angry as hell for having soaked a pack of Pall Malls and ruined his matches.

Jerry shook his head and moved his thoughts back to the hatchery. In his childhood, the entire place was made up of just a few long rectangular concrete bins dug into the earth and holding thousands of growing fish, awaiting their turn to be dumped into Lake Michigan or one of the inland lakes.

Now, the hatchery is more like a Jurassic Pond with a two mile walking trail lined by enormous majestic pine trees and flanked by somewhat recently constructed or enhanced ponds and streams. Along the way is a stop where one can actually walk down steps to below water level and watch the fish frolic in their human-made 'natural environment'.

Jerry spent a half hour or so walking the trails. This new hatchery bore zero resemblance to the one cradled in his early memory of the place, but it still brought back images of Lucy and Anne trying to convince Harry and Jerry that an hour of trout watching was more than enough on any given day.

On his way back to the parking lot, Jerry made a final stop at the underwater viewing station, hoping to get a glimpse of a small rainbow trout or two. Instead, he found himself nose to nose with the biggest brown trout he had ever seen. It was like the trout was viewing him, as he was viewing it. Both made fish faces at each other, opening and closing their mouths fishy-fashion less than an inch from the glass.

The fish was absolutely fine with the exchange, but Jerry was a bit embarrassed when a ten-year-old boy in a Detroit Tigers cap asked his dad, "What is that weird man doing?"

"Let's go, Dale," the father said as he pulled his son by the arm back up into the sunshine.

Jerry continued to stare at the trout. He thought of a sign Harry had hung in his first Detroit bar. It was written on a thin cross section of wood cut from a small tree trunk and read: *'Even a fish wouldn't get in trouble if he kept his mouth shut.'*

It was a good way to try to defuse arguments between semi or totally drunk factory workers. Jerry thought it might be good advice in the pond as well, so he shared it with his new friend, the brown trout. The trout wasn't impressed and just slowly turned and swam away.

"Don't say I didn't warn you," Jerry tapped on the glass. "Gotta go, buddy. Watch out for hookers!"

Turning to leave, Jerry was very grateful that Rob, or anyone else for that matter, had not been present to hear his final exchange with a trout.

Back at the parking lot, Jerry stepped into the visitors' center and walked up to one of the guides, a woman who looked to be about his age, with sparkling deep green eyes and a genuine smile.

"Excuse, me," Jerry smiled back. "But when did all this happen?"

"All what happen?"

"This whole place. It wasn't here a while back, just some concrete vats full of fish."

The woman nodded. "Pretty different, huh? Those vats, as you call them, were used from 1921 to 2002. That was when 'all this' happened."

The guide was about to launch into her practiced history of the hatchery, but Jerry was on a mission and, perhaps more importantly, beginning to develop a desperate need to pee. "Sorry to interrupt, but can I ask you two questions?"

"You can ask three," the woman's smile was now accompanied by a graceful, if somewhat flirtatious wink. She had noticed Jerry's eyes and smile. She liked both. She held out her hand. "I'm Edina."

"Jerry," he took her hand and held it for, perhaps, a second too long.

"But that wasn't one of my questions," Jerry quickly added.

"OK, consider it a freebie. Question 1? I am all ears," Edina gently touched both of her ears. She paused for a moment before saying, "Well, *mostly* all ears."

So cute, Jerry thought before getting back to his original first question, "Do you know what happened to The Hub?"

"What's the hub?" *So cute,* Edina thought. She casually glanced down at Jerry's left hand. *And single.*

"The Hub was a bar/restaurant just down the road from here toward Petoskey. Looked like a house? White? Kinda reddish roof. It even had a little strip motel of six, seven rooms, something like that."

"You called it The Hub?"

"Yeah, it was right on Crooked Lake."

"When I got here," Edina paused to calculate when she had moved Up North. "Must be 11 or 12 years ago now, there was some bar down the road in that direction but it wasn't The Hub," Edina ran her fingers through her hair.

"What was it called?"

"I think it was something like Lauer's, or Lauters, Lauders or something. It was totally run down and kind of a mess to tell you the truth. But now that I'm thinking about it, the place did look like it might have originally been an old house."

"That has to be it." Jerry smiled. "Where exactly was it?"

"It's where the Shores condos are now. You can't miss it."

I already miss it, Jerry thought.

"Now, what's your second question?"

Jerry suddenly felt a painful reminder of what now had become an almost exquisite need to urinate. It was high time that he asked his second question.

"Question two," Jerry's voice kind of squeaked out the question as he put his knees together and bit his lower lip. "Where's the men's room?"

Edina giggled. "Easier question, and fortunately for you I have the answer." She pointed to her right. "Second door down."

"Thank you."

When Jerry returned, relieved and ready for the next step in the great 'Hub Hunt', the guide was talking to the boy and his father who had witnessed the moment he had shared with the brown trout. When they saw him, the boy moved closer to his dad who put his arm around his son's shoulder.

"Excuse me for a moment." Edina smiled her lovely and inviting smile. "I'll be right back."

"They saw me communicating with a fish," Jerry gestured toward the father and son as Edina reached him halfway toward the door to the parking lot.

"Happens quite a bit around here," Edina said. "Meanwhile, you know you still have one more question. Remember, I promised you three answers."

"But I only had two questions."

The woman handed Jerry her card. "Maybe you'll think of something."

As Edina turned and walked back, intentionally slowly, towards the father and son, a number of intriguing, if somewhat salacious, questions did come to mind. Jerry put the card in his pocket and headed for the Jeep.

It didn't take long to drive to where The Hub used to be; in fact, in less than two minutes, Jerry arrived at the condominium complex that once was the site of his father's second life's dream. His first had come true when he returned from the war apparently intact and started his civilian married live with Lucy. Years later that first dream cancelled out the second, but Harry, certainly, would not have traded one for the other.

Turning in the driveway, Jerry stopped for a few seconds to stare at the gray stone sign set on light bricks that read: *'The Shores'*. To most people, the sign simply identified the condo complex. To Jerry, it looked more like a cemetery monument for the past. In his mind, Jerry saw the words: *'Here lie the remains of the Hub. May it rest in peace.'*

# # #

In Connecticut, Lucy lined up photographs of Harry, Jerry, Anne, and her mom on the table in front of her. She glanced at the calendar at the far end of the table. "July 12th," she whispered to Harry's image. "He must be there by now, honey; at The Hub. He must be."

She turned to the photo of her mom: "Will you help him, Mom? Please help him. Please help both of them."

While the eyes of Lucy's mom in the old picture continued to sparkle and smile, Lucy, now some 20 years older than her mom had been when she died, could still see the tears that had flowed from them when she learned her daughter was pregnant with Tommy.

Her mom was not 'peeved' about Lucy being pregnant. She was terrified. Lucy's news took her back to 1918 Poland, and the day her infant daughter Ursula and husband Casmir died.

# # #

Some 500 million people got the Spanish flu during the outbreak; about a third of the entire population of the planet. Upwards of 50 million people died. Casmir died at 2:11 in the morning while holding his young wife's hand. Six hours later, three-month-old Ursula had long since lost the strength to cry. With a final weak sob, she grasped her mother's finger one last time as Felicia gently rocked her precious baby girl in the carved rosewood rocking chair with its worn, brown leather upholstered seat.

Those were the two images that struck Lucy's mom when her daughter told her the news about Tommy. But in a very short period of time, the scars of the past were covered by the excitement of possibly being a grandmother.

Felicia Buraczynski didn't tell her daughter about what had happened in Poland in 1918 until the day Lucy lost Tommy on an operating table at Woman's Hospital in Detroit.

# # #

Lucy hugged all four photographs together. If her mom hadn't gone through the tragedy in that tiny Polish village, it is possible that she and her children would never have been born.

It was after the deaths that Felicia agreed to join her sister, Sabina, in the United States of America. Sabina later became known by all as Ciocia Babcia; Auntie Grandma.

# # #

When Lucy gave birth to Anne, her mom had cried tears of pure joy and golden sorrow. She held Harry by both cheeks so hard that his jaw hurt and said: "You are now a father and not a little boy. And I am finally a grandmother. We are complete."

When Jerry was born several years later, she had simply said to her son-in-law, "A boy! Go get drunk."

# # #

Jerry didn't get out of the car at the Shores. He just drove down the length of the parking lot, unable to even get a glimpse of Crooked Lake.

"Okay, enough. Next stop, Mitchell Street Pub," he said as he pulled past the tombstone and turned left back on to 31. He suddenly realized he was hungry…and thirsty.

Chapter 7

While it seems as though the earnest Mr. Hemingway drank in just about every bar or pub across every continent, except maybe Antarctica, Jerry thought he would have happily selected the Mitchell Street Pub in Petoskey for boozing it up, bullshitting, and creative inspiration. As soon as Jerry walked into the bar, he thought the author might actually still be haunting the place, but in all likelihood, no one would even notice.

The dark paneled walls were lined with bookshelves holding hardcover volumes in some areas and dead stuffed mammals, fish, birds, and possibly a reptile or two in others. In between was a wild plethora of antique advertising signs for things, like the one reading, *'Goodrich Rubbers'* and featuring a cat wearing waterproof rubber shoe coverings on each paw.

There were also street signs, an African shield, a barber pole, and a rusty shovel, each attached here and there to the walls and ceiling with no apparent rhyme or reason. A (presumably) disarmed military bomb, with a saddle strapped on in proper Dr. Strangelove fashion, dangled precariously from the rafters. Behind the long, shiny, early 20th-century-style oak saloon bar was a giant moose head wearing a baseball cap and enormous sun glasses. Alongside Bullwinkle were signs reading *'If you are grouchy, irritable, or just plain mean, there will be a $10 dollar charge for putting up with you'* and another saying that *'Jesus would slap the shit out of you.'*

An ornate, flashy, and brightly multi-color lit jukebox looked like it was straight out of the 1940s. One could easily imagine every person in the bar suddenly leaping to their feet to jitterbug to the swing band sounds of Benny Goodman, Glenn Miller, or Cab Calloway. In his mind, Jerry clearly heard Duke Ellington's band trumpeting out, "It don't mean a thing if you ain't got that swing."

Peanut shells littered the floor and the aroma of beer and deep fried everything filled the air. It seemed as if every inch of the place held something that you could talk about, argue over, laugh at, or find plain old disgusting. Jerry loved it.

While Mitchell Street offered tables and booths, with red checkered table cloths which were serviced by appropriately cranky waitresses who had to put up with the din and dizzying atmosphere in order to make a living, Jerry pulled up a stool at one end of the bar, ordered a Labatt draft, and asked for a menu.

He smiled while reading what the Mitchell Street Pub had to offer. The menu fit right into the amazing and wonderful eclectic shit storm that was, is, and will probably always be the Mitchell Street Pub in Petoskey, Michigan.

What would Hemingway eat? Jerry thought as he started reading down the appetizer list that stretched from fried cheese curds and deep fried jalapeno poppers stuffed with cream cheese to shrimp jammers and fried batter-covered mushrooms served with a creamy horseradish sauce. The main courses included the self-proclaimed 'best on the planet' nachos, 'our famous' white chili and the 'best burger in town'.

I wonder why it's not the best burger on the planet? Jerry thought while reading on about the 'local favorite' chili dog, the 'EXTRAORDINARY' Reuben, and the grilled BBQ chicken sandwich that is so good that 'all our chickens are volunteers'.

There was also a nice list of soups and salads, but Jerry skipped that page.

"I'll have the mini tacos appetizer, B&B Burger (Pub burger topped with thick sliced bacon and melted bleu cheese), a side of fries and," *as a shout out to healthy eating,* "coleslaw!"

Before Jerry lost himself in the menu, there had only been a young man in a black Harley Davidson T-shirt and another wearing a 'Detroit vs. Everybody' hoodie sitting at the other end of the bar. But when he looked up again, the Millennials were gone, having been replaced by a scruffy-faced 40-ish man in a faded Johnson Outboard Motor cap with the visor in the shape of a U from having been pushed into the back pocket of his dirty khaki pants hundreds, if not thousands, of times.

The man's uncut and unkempt salt and pepper hair curled out in a tangle from beneath the cap, and he seemed to be intensely staring out at nothing in particular from under wild and bushy brown and white eyebrows that could also have used a clipping and probably a bit of soap and water.

Jerry couldn't take his eyes off the man, *He's the guy from the breakwater*, Jerry thought. *I know him from someplace.*

When the man noticed Jerry looking his way, he smiled, waved, and struggled to get up from his bar stool.

Damn it, he's coming over.

The man walked with a noticeable limp and kept his right hand on the bar for balance.

Drunk or disabled? Drunk and disabled?

"Hiya!" The man's voice was gravelly and contained a bit of a growl. He smelled like fish and whiskey. "Name's Eddie, Eddie Little." The man put out his hand. "Mind if I join ya?"

Without waiting for an answer, Eddie sat on the bar stool next to Jerry with a noticeable groan, as he stretched out his right leg.

Jerry hesitated before somewhat reluctantly taking his hand. "I'm, Jerry. And, ahh, I guess I don't mind."

"Yeah, I saw you looking over my way and I figured, what the holy hell, might as well have some company."

Eddie again groaned a bit, as he bent and straightened his leg three times, kicking Jerry in the shin twice during the process. "Oops, sorry about that. Leg's for shit ever since I got it all shot up and sloppy in the war."

"Iraq?"

"Okinawa."

# # #

Lucy put down the pictures and closed her eyes. She drifted back to that one particular 3 am in Petoskey. She remembered distinctly that it had been the 14th of July when Harry had told her who he met earlier at The Hub.

Quickly smelling his breath to see if he had been drinking, Lucy had said: "Harry, I wish you were drunk because that's crazy."

"Yep," Harry agreed. "Crazy in spades."

After telling her the whole story, Harry and Lucy had stood silently in the doorway to their son's bedroom watching young Jerry breathing peacefully in his sleep.

Back in present-day Connecticut, Lucy's eyes opened wide and she gasped for breath. She looked around the room, half expecting to see that she was in the bedroom at Mary's house Up North in Petoskey instead of in her assisted living apartment in Connecticut. "What a dream. What a dream."

It took several minutes, but finally her pulse slowed, and her present reality came back into focus. Her head, hip, knees, ankles, and ribs ached, as she rose from her seat. She remembered what her oldest and dearest friend Wanda had said about getting old. "Everything hurts and nothing works."

Wanda had passed away from a heart attack a couple of years earlier. After the unexpected death, Lucy had written up two lists of people that she knew, both friends and family. One list included those who were alive, and the other those who weren't. The 'weren't' list was much, much longer.

I have to do this, Lucy thought as she used her walker to carefully edge her way to the bathroom with its handicapped bath tub. She wanted to wash her hair more than she had in a very long time. Usually, one of the nursing assistants at the home would help her during the day with what had become a difficult and potentially dangerous process. As one ages, falling becomes a life-threatening hazard. But on this particular night, Lucy *needed* to wash her hair on her own because she wanted to look good for her darling hubby Harry in her dreams.

# # #

Meanwhile, at Mitchell Street, Eddie must have missed the confused look on Jerry's face regarding the answer he gave to his new friend's question about where he had been wounded. He just turned his cap backwards and kept on talking without missing a beat. "Yeah, I was a real gung ho motherfucker when I was younger."

"You were in the army?"

"Hell no, bunch of pussies in the Army. I'm Marine all the way." Eddie picked up the sleeve on his T-shirt to show a tattoo of an angry looking American bald eagle digging its talons into the planet Earth below. Above the bird was a scroll with the letters U.S.M.C.

"Semper fucking fi mother fucker. Semper fucking fi."

"What did you mean when you said 'Okinawa'?" Jerry asked.

Eddie changed the subject. "Where you from, Jerry boy? You sure ain't local."

Eddie didn't even wait for an answer to his own question. "Now you know, Jerry, it is a custom around here for any non-local pisser coming through to buy a local fella, particularly a wounded vet like say yours truly, a round or two to guarantee friendly-like relations."

"That so?"

"Yep, goes all the way back to the Indians and such. In fact, that's why the old Algonquin nation even let white folk settle into this place."

"Because they bought them drinks at the Mitchell Street Pub?"

"Yep, that's the legend."

Jerry smiled: "That's so bad."

"Yeah, I guess it is." Eddie laughed. "But do I get my shot and beer?"

"Sure," Jerry waved the bartender over.

"Come on, Georgie," Eddie called out. "Get your barkeeping ass in gear. I am dying of thirst over here."

Georgie was not the same bartender who had handed Jerry a menu moments earlier. *Must have been a shift change,* Jerry thought. *A really quick shift change.*

"Eddie," the bartender shook his head. "Are you at it again?"

"Yeah." Eddie slapped Jerry on the back and laughed even louder. "And it looks like I got myself a real live one here! Ain't that so, Jerry?"

Jerry now laughed as well. "Seems so," Jerry joined in the banter.

"*Seems* so," Eddie ordered a shot of Kessler's whiskey and a Pabst Blue Ribbon draft. "Now where did you say you was from? I know it's gotta be down south somewhere."

"I'm originally from Detroit."

"South enough for me."

Jerry left the subject, he really didn't want to hear Eddie's view of Detroit and certainly not of New York. "So, you grew up around here?"

"Whole fucking life. You might just say that I was born with a silver fishhook in my mouth."

Fishhook, Jerry thought. "Were you on the breakwater earlier today?"

"Maybe so, maybe no, don't really recall, doesn't really matter."

Whole fucking life. Jerry jumped at the opportunity. "Can I ask you a question; one you have to answer straight."

Eddie drained his whiskey. "Ahhh, like they say 'smooth as silk'."

He chugged his beer and belched. "Now I would be happy to answer your question if you showed an old Leatherneck a bit of hospitality." He looked at Jerry while pushing both glasses in his direction. "If you get my drift."

Jerry waved the bartender over. "I think my friend needs another."

Eddie belched again. "Shit yeah. You got that one right."

The bartender filled the shot glass to just below the rim. "You're getting kinda stingy there, ain't ya, Georgie?"

The bartender poured enough whiskey in the glass until it just ran over the top and onto the polished wood of the bar.

"That's better," Eddie leaned over and slurped the top layer of the whiskey from the glass. "I say it again; smooth as silk."

Eddie laughed and downed the rest of the shot. "Hey, you only live once, right Jer-O?"

Again, Eddie slapped Jerry on the back. But this time, Jerry didn't feel a thing.

Okay, too weird, Jerry thought. *Just find out what this crazy guy knows and get the fuck out of here.*

Meanwhile Eddie had slugged down half of his second beer and called out to the bartender; "Hey, Georgie Porgy, can you put a head on this? Seems to have gone flat."

He pushed the shot glass toward George, "And this little fella seems to have gone all empty."

"Eddie," George, the bartender, said, taking his shot glass and refilling the pilsner beer glass to the top. "Are you ever gonna stop this?"

"Hell no, I'll be haunting this place forever."

"Ain't that the truth?" George turned to Jerry. "Don't let this guy bamboozle you into buying all night long."

"Well, now, he gave away my plan!"

Another slap on the back without impact or sound. "No tip for you Georgie Porgie!"

Eddie pointed to his empty shot glass. "I gotta be careful not to get too soused or the little woman will use my balls for bait."

"Ain't much of a worry there," George said as he refilled Eddie's shot glass. "Won't be catchin' nothing with them. Fish around here prefer live bait."

"Ohhhhhh, Georgie Porgie, you made up a funny one there," Eddie looked down at the full shot glass, slugged it, and smiled.

George filled it up again.

"You are reading my mind."

"Yeah, like we're fucking soul mates, right?" George walked away.

Eddie turned to Jerry, who had started to worry about not feeling any sensation in his back.

Pinched nerve? Slipped disc? God forbid, worse?

"Now, you had a question and paid for an answer," Eddie brought Jerry back to the story gathering task at hand. "What do you want to know?"

"Hub Bar." Jerry got right to the point.

"Yeah, what about it?" Eddie asked.

"You heard of it?"

"Son, there ain't a bar this side of Cheboygan that I ain't heard about, shit in, or been thrown out of."

"But do you know what happened to it?'

"What happened to it?"

"Yeah," Jerry said. "You know, when they built the condos?"

"The what—*dos*?" Eddie laughed. "I heard of con*doms*, but not *dos*. You sure you got your rubber on right?"

"Come on, Eddie," Jerry was getting a bit annoyed. "Be serious. The Shores condominiums that they built where The Hub used to be."

"Used to be?" Now it was Eddie's turn to look at Jerry, as if he had more than a single screw loose. "Man, I thought I was the one dead drunk around here."

"I'm not drunk," Jerry was tired of this guy's game. "I was up there not an hour and a half ago and The Hub is gone."

"You must be shitfaced. I was just there last night. Got all snockered up, if you can believe that. Love The Hub! They got a new part-time bartender there. Guy's from the south, just like you. Sings like a son of a biscuit, but he loaned me ten bucks without even knowing me from Adam. My kind of guy!"

"What are you talking about?"

"Tell you what, friend," Eddie smiled. "Let's not get all pissy-ass and fight about it. Let's go up there and drink about it. Listen, if we go there and The Hub ain't fucking there, I'll stop drinking for all eternity. But if it is there, and it *is* there, drinks for the whole night are on you."

"Alright, then let's go," Jerry thought he could hear more of this guy's story as they drove to the Shores.

"Ahh, not tonight."

"Figures."

"Nah, I got lots of shit to do tonight. Let's go the day after Friday."

"Saturday?"

"That works for me."

"Okay," Jerry said. "When and where do you want to meet?"

"How about here, say 4 o'clock or so?" Eddie said. "You got a vehicle of some kind, 'cause you sure as shittin' don't want me to drive."

"Fine, I'll be here at 4."

"Oh," Eddie rubbed his hands together. "Hub's gonna be a-hoppin' on Saturday. Good we're going to get there way early before the place fills up."

"Eddie…" Jerry was going to again tell this strange man that there is no Hub, only condos, when his new 'friend' interrupted him.

"Here comes your food," Eddie nodded toward a waitress carrying a tray toward them behind the bar. "Bon appetite!"

"You don't mind that I brought it all at once, do you?" The waitress laid Jerry's entire order before him on the bar. "Saves me a trip."

Jerry looked down at his food. When he looked up, the waitress was walking away and the first bartender was back at the other end of the bar serving a young man in a Harley Davidson T-shirt and another in a 'Detroit vs. Everybody' hoodie. The bar next to him was empty, polished, and dry. Eddie was gone, but the stool he was sitting on turned slowly clockwise before coming to a stop.

"Everything OK here?" The original bartender had walked over after seeing that his customer wasn't touching his food and had the expression of a deer in car headlights. "Food alright? You alright?"

"Yeah, fine," Jerry picked up a fry and popped it into his mouth. "What happened to the other bartender?"

"Just me, friend. Until the clock strikes two, and I am through."

"By the way," Jerry tried to sound as casual as possible. "I was just here with some guy named Eddie. Did you see him leave?"

"Eddie," the bartender sighed a disgusted sigh, threw a towel over his arm and walked away muttering, "Not him again."

# # #

In Connecticut, Lucy put on lipstick and went to bed. She kissed the pillow beside her, leaving a lip print just like the ones she ended every letter with during the war. "Good night, Harry. Love you forever."

Chapter 8

By the time Jerry got back to the Apple Tree, Rob was filled with pepperoni pizza and happily dozing off on the couch in his room. He was startled awake by the loud knocking on his door. Jerry just couldn't wait to tell him what had happened.

Rob's reaction? "And you're going to meet this wacko on Saturday? On purpose?"

"Yeah, man, don't you think it's weird?"

Rob yawned. "Why is it exactly that we are here?"

"On Earth?"

"In Petoskey."

"To relax, show you northern Michigan, have fun."

"Is that what we're doing?"

Jerry thought about his answer before saying: "I don't know what's happening, I really don't. But I sure find it interesting."

"Can we pick up on 'interesting' in the morning?" Rob made it abundantly clear that it was time for Jerry to head back down the hallway to his own room. "And, *no*, egg-eyes in meatloaf are not interesting."

"To a seven-year-old, they are."

"Exactly," Rob guided Jerry calmly, but firmly to the door. "Get some sleep. You sound like you've been smoking something all night long."

Smoking, Jerry thought a short while later, as he sat on his balcony watching the green blinking light from Harbor Springs flash across the bay. He sipped a glass of wine and dreamed of the days when he would have enjoyed several cigarettes to add to the experience.

Wouldn't be here now if I had kept smoking, Jerry thought. *That's a fucking fact. But it sure was fun.*

Jerry once smoked three packs a day, although, his Vantage cigarettes didn't compare at all in strength to Harry's unfiltered Pall Malls, or later Lucy's Larks that had a slight taste of honey when inhaled.

A reaction to a spider bite had sent Jerry to Beaumont Hospital in Royal Oak, Michigan some 25 years earlier, at which point the doctor tossed him into ICU and blamed smoking.

They kept him in Intensive Care for two days and in the cardiac unit for two more, during which time Jerry had kept pointing at the obvious red spot where the spider had chowed down, a fact ignored by doctors, nurses, candy girls and others. They all insisted that the incident probably revolved around smoking. "Okay," Jerry finally figured. "Why don't I just quit."

Two and a half decades later, he still missed smoking every day. He also remembered what Rob had said once about starting smoking being a 'celebration of life' and quitting smoking being exactly the same thing. "You start smoking when you think you're never gonna die; you quit smoking when you know you will. It's all about life."

Now, of course, Rob had taken a toke or two of marijuana when he made his profound pronouncement, but that didn't really matter a whole bunch to Jerry at the time because he had joined his friend in his pipe dream. After the epiphany about life and smoking, the two men had eaten a full bag of Oreo cookies and microwaved a 16-piece pack of frozen White Castle cheeseburgers.

Jerry smiled at the memory, got up from his chair on the balcony, and walked slowly to his bed. Before drifting off, he said, "Goodnight, Mom. See you in the morning," as he'd done so many times before.

When Lucy lived with Jerry to help when Amanda was little, Jerry would knock softly on the wall separating their bedrooms every night. The knock would come after Jerry had finished reading Amanda several books, her positive sleeping status had been firmly established, and he had succeeded in tiptoeing silently from her room to his own.

"Goodnight, Mom, see you in the morning," Jerry would say softly, but loud enough for Lucy to hear. It was a signal that it was safe for the adults to call it a night. The knock and sign-off became a tradition over the years, and it always made Lucy smile.

For Jerry, when Lucy answered, "See you in the morning," it served as confirmation that a morning there would, in fact, be. *After all,* Jerry would often think before closing his eyes and slipping into sleep, *my mom says so.*

# # #

When their dad died, Anne and Jerry had a private rib dinner in his honor. Lucy said she had to deal with visiting relatives, so she couldn't make it, but the brother and sister savored every bite and 3 a.m. memory of their dad, their mom, their family.

With every 'do you remember when...' and 'do you remember how...' they would laugh and offer differing perspectives on the same event. It was fascinating how while they shared common events, their lasting memories of those moments would often be as different as night and day. There were also things that one of them would remember clearly and the other not have the faintest recollection of at all.

What they did share completely was the knowledge that while there were plenty of family traumas and dramas, they always knew that their parents loved them. "You know," Anne said, "we were really lucky. I know so many people, friends, who went through real hell with their parents."

"Like Dad," Jerry said.

"Yeah," Anne agreed. "He never would talk about them."

"Maybe he couldn't," Jerry paused. "Or maybe he was ashamed of them."

"Or maybe he didn't want us to see how angry and hurt he really was."

"That sounds like Dad."

Anne nodded. "The more people I talk to, the more I understand that we did have two really good parents who loved us and each other."

"Yeah," Jerry agreed. "I read once that a person doesn't really become a grown-up until both parents are gone. Until then, we are still children, still feeling safe, or I guess in some cases tortured when they're around. While they're alive, we can still call or scream out to Mommy and Daddy."

"Well, to our daddy," Anne raised a French fry, Jerry did the same with a rib.

"A good father," Jerry paid his dad what he thought was, perhaps, the best compliment a father could ever get. He remembered whispering to Amanda when she was only a few hours old. "I'll try to be good daddy. I promise to try really hard."

"A good father." Anne agreed. "We love you Dad."

Jerry hid his emotions by quickly scarfing down half a slice of garlic bread and changing the subject. "Hey, Anne, do you remember the Circle C?"

The Circle C was an 'Up North' memory that both Anne and Jerry shared. It was the moment of proof that the Piaseckis would never be cowboys. Harry had come up with the idea for a family horse riding adventure after talking to a guy at The Hub.

Lucy wasn't too keen on the thought of saddling up. "Harry, honey, have you ever been on a horse?"

"What's the big deal?" Harry laughed. "You park your fanny in the saddle and go."

"If you say so, Harry."

"I also bought these," Harry pulled four Texas style cowboy hats out of a giant brown paper bag. "This is going to be great. I just have one question."

"What's that?"

"How do you say giddy-up in Polish?"

Circle C was a riding stable about ten miles outside of Petoskey. All went pretty well when the family got on their mounts near the hardened dirt parking lot. Jerry rode an Appaloosa, Anne a brown and white pinto, Lucy a brown horse with a darker brown mane, and Harry a black horse named Fury.

The event ended shortly after it began with Lucy's horse stopping after about 20 yards to leisurely and adamantly eat grass. Anne fell off her horse and ran back to the car. Jerry's steed chose to wander into the woods, and Harry's Fury simply turned around and sauntered oh-so-slowly back into the barn.

When the family finally got back into the car for the ride home to Petoskey, Harry said; "Let's try it again next week."

Three other voices in the car chorused as one: "Noooooooo!"

Lucy 'lost' her cowboy hat when it 'accidentally' flew out the car window, Anne had left hers in the dirt, and Jerry forgot his in Petoskey that summer. Harry, on the other hand, proudly displayed his at the 7 Mile Hub back in Detroit. He loved telling stories about his riding prowess, while claiming to be the Polish John Wayne.

Chapter 9

"Just a quick stop where The Hub was, okay? Then it's off to Mackinaw," Jerry had called Rob's room at 6 a.m. the next morning, an hour and a half before the wake-up call Rob had left at the front desk.

Rob looked at the clock. "Jerry, I have a thought."

"Yeah."

"Can I kill you?" he closed his eyes. "Hmmm?"

"Rob! Not nice!"

"Okay, okay, okay. Can I *please* kill you?"

"Come on man, how often are you Up North."

"I'm starting to think way too often."

"We've got to get moving!" Jerry woke up full speed and ready for whatever the day might bring. He even thought of suggesting that they go horseback riding but quickly thought better of it. Still, he was excited about the plan to show Rob Mackinaw Island, which would put them on course to pass where The Hub bar and restaurant used to be. He also somehow thought that passing The Shores might help him make a final determination on the emotional status of Eddie and whether he would meet him or not.

"I am telling you, man," Jerry said. "I am full of piss and vinegar this morning."

"Now there's a phrase that should never have been written." Rob fell back on to his pillow.

"You know it comes from a John Steinbeck novel from the 30s I think, but he probably got it from…"

"Oh just shut the fuck up!" Rob put his pillow over his face and screamed into the telephone: "Coffee!"

"Okay, coffee first. So no one can say I'm being unreasonable."

Rob hung up.

Jerry and Rob picked up large coffees and, according to Jerry, the 'best blueberry muffins on the planet' from the bakery across from the hospital. It was a crisp and clear morning, perfect for enjoying breakfast at the end of the breakwater.

"You know, I could have enjoyed the muffins just as much in bed," Rob said as they pulled into one of the visitors parking spaces. "In bed and closer to say, oh I don't know, noon?"

"Nah, this is better. Come on. Let's go."

As Jerry led the way down the 900-or-so-foot breakwater, Rob knew his friend was correct. On his left, two to three-foot waves hit against the concrete barrier, splashing up and crashing over the top at times, sending mist to the other side. On his right, the water was still—without ripple or wrinkle. When they stood at the very end, Rob saw the waves pass uninterrupted and unbroken before gently rolling on toward the far shore, sparing the marina from any possibility of harm.

"I can see why you love it up here." Rob took a bite from his blueberry muffin. "Damn," some of the muffin crumbs tumbled from his mouth. "These *are* great muffins!"

Jerry kept staring out at the horizon just as he did decades earlier. If you looked at anything touched by human hands over those same years, the changes were obvious. *Not when things are touched only by the hand of God,* Jerry thought. *Eternity doesn't change. It just is.*

"Ahh, Jer," Rob said with some urgency. "I think we have guests for breakfast."

Snapping back to the muffins at hand, Jerry looked down to see that he and Rob had been joined by a dozen sea gulls, not one of them too shy to let his or her presence and her or his desires known.

"Watch this." Jerry had bought a couple of extra muffins, remembering something his dad had shown him when he was seven years old. As he crumbled the muffins in both hands, the gulls started to screech and move in closer for the crumbs. He then tossed the muffin pieces into the water before him, causing the gulls to pause for a 10th of a second before, as if as one, diving straight down into the water for their treat.

"They can fight it out with the fish," Jerry said, hearing Harry say the exact same words. Sure enough, not three or four seconds later, several of the gulls were bopped from below by some finned-fellows who also wanted a morning muffin munchie.

In a flash, all of the floating muffin jetsam was devoured, with one lucky gull flying off with most of the muffin top. The remaining gulls looked up at Jerry, who emptied the rest of the crumbs from the bag. "We better get out of here before they realize we are without muffin and of no practical use to them anymore," he laughed.

As they walked back down the breakwater, Rob put his arm around Jerry's shoulder. "You know what my favorite part of this morning has been?"

"What?"

"You didn't see any of those fishy ghosty guys you've been talking about."

Jerry stopped and looked back toward the end of the breakwater. All he saw were four seagulls slowly walking after them. Picking up their pace toward the car, Jerry responded to Rob's observation. "You're right. No fishy ghosty guys. Not yet anyway."

Less than 15 minutes later, Jerry pointed to the Shores condominiums slowing down slightly as he drove by on their way to Mackinaw. "That's where The Hub was."

"*Was* is the operative word, Jer. That guy you talked to last night was either drunk, drugged up, or just plain old wacked out."

"Yeah, I guess so."

"Guess so?" Rob shook his head. "You *guess* so?"

When Jerry mumbled some intentionally incomprehensible response Rob said, "You're not gonna meet up with him on Saturday, are you?"

Jerry watched the speedometer rise from 65 to 80 miles per hour.

"Are you?" Rob repeated the question just as the car zoomed toward and then past the fish hatchery on the left.

"Look, Rob, look! That's the fish hatchery I told you about. I wonder if Edina's working today."

"God, you *are* going to meet him."

"Don't know." Jerry's attempt to change the subject to either fish or Edina had failed. "Maybe so, maybe no."

Why did I use Eddie's phrase? Jerry thought. *And why the fuck am I hearing his voice saying it in my head?*

"Jer, the guy's nuts."

"But interesting."

"I bet Jack the Ripper and Charlie Manson were *interesting*, but I sure wouldn't want to be having a chat with them over drinks. And I definitely would not want to be alone with them in my car."

"Nothing to worry about there, Rob. Nothing at all."

"Why not?"

"Because you'll be in the back seat."

"Oh great, maybe I'll bring my guitar, so I can try to strum some sense into the man."

"Well, you did learn '*Hopelessly Midwestern*'."

Rob shook his head. "You know I'm going to try to talk you out of all this nonsense, don't you?"

"How you gonna do it?"

"We'll see." Rob looked out the passenger side window as they drove past the couple blocks of small stores on US 31 that made up Alanson, Michigan (Population pushing 750 on a good day). "I have about 48 hours to figure something out."

Jerry turned right on 68 to cut over to I 75. He could get to Mackinaw by staying on US 31, but he felt hitting the big highway was the fastest way there, and when Mackinaw Island fudge is a-calling, speed is of the essence.

# # #

When Anne arrived at her mom's place at 11 that morning, she found Lucy sitting in her favorite straight back chair dressed in a gray wool skirt, purple blouse, and multi-colored scarf. Her now white hair was clean and brushed straight back. She was in full makeup, and while her lipstick was a bit smudged and her eye liner a little out of line, (Lucy's hands weren't as steady as they once were) Anne knew her mom had done her best, for whatever reason she had for doing it at all.

"Why are you all dressed up, Mom?" Anne asked. "Some event in the building?"

"No," Lucy straightened her skirt. "Just felt like it. I guess I wanted to look good for a change."

"Mom, you always, look good."

"You are such a little liar," Lucy smiled at her oldest child. "I love you for it. In fact, I love you more."

"Not more than I love you," Anne carried on the tradition of having a dialogue containing the lines: "I love you", "I love you more", "No, I love YOU more", etc.

Finally Anne broke the pattern by making an '*I love you more*' peace offering. "Here, Mom, I brought you a sundae from Carvel. Strawberry sundae with vanilla ice cream, nuts, whipped cream, and…"

"…a cherry." Lucy completed the sentence and held out both hands for the white paper bag that held her treat. "Perfect, just like Dad used to bring me from Sweetland."

"Just like that." Anne pulled the sundae and pink plastic spoon from the bag. Sitting on the couch next to the chair, Anne just watched her mom enjoy her sundae memories.

When Lucy was half way through, she put the sundae on the coffee table, closed her eyes, and took several deep breaths.

"Mom, are you alright?"

"Oh, yes," she smiled without opening her eyes. "Anne, you know I was just thinking, I might not be beautiful, or even pretty, but every time your father looked at me, I felt like the most beautiful girl in the world."

Chapter 10

Mackinac Island—even the most hardened New Yorker, you know the ones who think anything west of the Hudson River is of no consequence to civilized society, has heard of Mackinac Island. The palatial Grand Hotel, with its 660-foot geranium-lined front porch and Esther Williams swimming pool in the shape of Paul Bunyan's boot print, has hosted millions of guests ranging from the likes of Mark Twain to President Kennedy; Madonna to Ruth Bader Ginsberg.

"You know the movie *'Somewhere in Time'* was filmed at the Grand Hotel back in '79," Jerry shouted out the information so that Rob could hear it over the engines of the small ferry boat that bounced hard from wave to wave. Most of those traveling to the Island took shelter in the covered area of the ferry, but Jerry thought it would be fun to ride it out on deck. The only way to the Island is by ferry, small plane, or helicopter.

"Hey, Rob, look, the Mackinac Bridge." Jerry pointed straight out to the long bridge in the distance connecting Michigan's Lower and Upper Peninsulas. "That sucker is about 5 miles long. My family was up here on the day it opened. It scared the hell out of me to drive over it as a kid. Kept my eyes closed, and my dad laughing all the way across."

Rob wasn't interested in any bridge no matter how spectacular. He was too busy focusing on holding down his muffin.

"Woo whooo! Here comes a big one, man!" Jerry yelled a moment before a five-foot wave broke over the bow, soaking the two men to the bone.

Rob turned various shades of green, as Jerry rambled on about how while the Island had about an equal number of permanent residents and horses (500 or so each), over a million tourists visit the place each year. The locals call the tourists Fudgies.

Jerry had carefully Googled his Mackinac facts which he recited dutifully to his groaning friend. "No cars on the Island, only horses, buggies, and bikes. The Grand Hotel is an official National Historic Landmark. And don't get me started on the fudge."

At the very thought of 'fudge', Rob collapsed off the bench he and Jerry were sitting on and spent the rest of the 20-minute voyage holding his stomach and curled up in a tight ball on the deck.

Jerry suggested going inside the ferry's cabin, to which Rob could only reply by moaning: "I can't move. I can't move. I can't move. I can't move," over and over again.

It took about a half hour for Rob to get his land-legs once the ferry docked on the Island. He spent the time flat on his back on a grassy rise of land near the boats. Within a few minutes, he started to feel somewhat normal, although, it did take the full half hour for the rocking sensation to stop completely.

Jerry had wandered off into town only to return with a book about the ghosts of Mackinac. "Look what I found at one of the stores. This is so cool."

"What is it?" Rob had his right arm over his eyes to block the sun.

"A book."

"Which book?"

"A ghosts of Mackinac book. It says that the Grand Hotel I told you about is considered the most haunted hotel in Michigan."

"Did you bring me here to chase ghosts?" Rob kept his eyes covered.

"No," Jerry said honestly. "You know I wouldn't have done that to you."

Rob got up and let his eyes adjust to the light. "But that's all you seem to be doing, chasing ghosts."

"Not true. If anything they seem to be chasing me."

Rob slowly shook his head and started walking away. "How's about we just go riding? Does that work for you?"

97

"You mean, like, riding *bikes*, right?" Jerry quickly got up and followed.

"You want to ride horses?"

"Bikes are good." Jerry said quickly as he caught up to Rob. "But don't you want to hear about the evil spirit in the theater or the cigar smoking ghost in a top hat at the piano bar?"

"Fuck no!"

"How about the Victorian woman who gets into bed with staff members."

Rob slowed down just a bit and paused: "Maybe later."

M-185 is the safest highway in the United States, if not the world. It is the only highway in the U.S. where motor vehicles are banned by law. In fact, only emergency gas powered vehicles are allowed on the Island at all. It took Jerry and Rob about two and a half hours to bike the 8.3 miles around the island because of stops to either admire the scenery or grab a beer.

By the time they completed the trek, it was almost time to head back to the mainland before the bats of Mackinac burst forth in their evening ritual.

"Fudge first?" Jerry asked.

Rob's intestines churned slightly from the memory of the ferry, but on the other hand, the thought of the island's famous treat was appealing on some digestive level as well. "Sure, when in Mackinaw do as a 'fudgie' do."

"Yep," Jerry agreed. "Fudgie and proud of it!"

"What the hell is a 'penuche'?" Rob scratched his head as he looked down the long glass case holding about every type of designer fudge one could imagine.

"Actually, that's one I know," Jerry looked equally baffled. When he was there decades earlier with Harry, Lucy, and Anne, there had only been chocolate, vanilla, and penuche (maple) fudge. The single complication was whether to have it with or without nuts. Now, some two dozen fudges demanded attention and deserved to be savored. Turtle fudge, amaretto cherry fudge, Butterfinger fudge, sea salt caramel fudge.

Both Rob and Jerry remembered their 'smoking and life' discussion when their gaze settled on the Oreo fudge, but then they were distracted by pumpkin spice and candy cane twist. There was frosted fudge, coconut covered fudge, and fudge topped with sprinkles both common and rare.

Jerry was dazed and confused when the store clerk asked for his order. Knowing he had only two choices; the first being 'everything' which seemed unrealistic, Jerry took choice number two. 'Chocolate'.

"Nuts or no nuts?"

Jerry walked out of the store with both. Rob couldn't make up his mind and settled for peanut brittle.

Rob breathed a deep sigh of relief when he and Jerry got aboard the ferryboat for the return trip to Mackinac City on the mainland. Now, Lake Huron was as smooth as glass, with the only ripple coming from the wake of the boat as it pushed through the silken stillness of the water. Rob happily ate his peanut brittle while Jerry regretted not ordering the bear claw fudge that contained chocolate liqueur processed with alkali, whatever that meant.

Driving back in the Jeep toward Petoskey, neither man said a word. Jerry seemed lost in thought while Rob nibbled at his brittle and then at some of Jerry's chocolate fudge with nuts. As they approached the Shores condominium complex on the left, Jerry slowed and stared at the place. For a brief moment in his mind, he saw it as it had been, actually feeling the brass handle on The Hub's bright red door. The smell of his dad's Old Spice aftershave filled the car.

"Jer! Look out!" Rob screamed from the passenger seat.

Before Jerry could turn, he felt the car hit something hard. First the loud thud came from the front of the car and then something bounced first off the hood and then the roof.

"What the fuck was that?" Jerry jammed on the brakes and pulled the car over.

"I have no fucking idea!" Rob slammed the dashboard with both hands.

"Was it a deer?" Jerry had squeezed the steering wheel so hard that it left an impression on the palms of his hands.

"That was no deer," Rob had leaned forward, putting his head on his hands.

"Then what the hell was it?" Jerry didn't wait for an answer before getting out of the car and looking back down the road, expecting to see whatever it was he had hit.

"Shit, that can't be." The road was empty and clean except for a couple of passing cars and the skid marks left from his own tires.

Staring at the Shores, Jerry again saw it morph momentarily into The Hub. This time though, his dad was standing at the door looking directly at the Jeep. It was as if he had come out to see what all the ruckus was about.

Jerry closed his eyes and counted to three. When he opened them, his dad's face was inches away from his own. Harry's mouth was moving as if asking a question, but Jerry couldn't hear what he was saying.

He closed his eyes again, only to open them a moment later when he heard Rob say: "Jer, let's get out of here." Now it was Rob's face directly in front of his. Jerry looked back at the Shores and then back at his friend.

"*Now* would be as good a time as any," Rob insisted. "Let's go!

Jerry didn't argue.

They hadn't gone a mile down the road before Jerry turned to his friend. "What did you see back there? What did we hit?"

Rob just stared straight ahead. "Man, I don't know. We were driving by those condos and as soon as you looked over at them there suddenly, I can't even describe it, something like smoke, but solid smoke right in front of the car. That's what we hit. I thought maybe it was a bear or something, birds maybe or a huge swarm of bugs. But then, there was nothing."

"And not a dent or even a scratch on the car." Jerry tightened his grip on the steering wheel. "Damn."

"Yeah, but there has to be some logical explanation." Rob's mind was starting to take over the matter. "It just had to be some kind of birds, or bugs or I don't know, maybe a tarp or something blew free in the wind."

"You think we hit a tarp?"

"You got a better idea?"

"Did you see my dad?" Jerry asked matter-of-factly.

"Oh, come on man," Rob sighed. "You don't think you saw your father?"

"Saw something."

After a minute or so of silence, Rob asked. "Jer, can you do me a favor and just stop all this nonsense?"

Jerry had to fight the instinct to immediately say two simple words: "Sure, OK." Those words seemed both so very right and so very wrong. "You're right. It is getting weird, I'll give you that."

"Weird?"

"Yeah, weird."

"Jer, you are having drinks with fucking wack jobs, seeing fisher-guy-ghosts that ain't there, running into solid black smoke on a clear road, and seeing your dad at a bar that's a condo development."

"Yeah." Jerry had to smile. "Weird all right."

"But if you don't just cut it out, I think weird might turn into crazy."

"I don't know, Rob. It just seems like everything is happening for a reason."

"And what might that reason be?"

"I have no fucking idea." Jerry was getting a headache. He knew his friend was probably right.

"Then be reason-able, Jer. Let it go. Or at least, let it go tomorrow and think about whether you should really meet up with that freak Eddie on Saturday or not. Let tomorrow be a freak-free day and let's do what we were supposed to do up here."

"You know, Rob, I really don't know any more why we came here."

"We came here to drink and meet women."

"We do that in New York."

"And your point is exactly what?"

Jerry thought about what Rob had said. He really had no idea what was happening. Coming up to Petoskey was supposed to be a trip down memory lane, and a chance to show his friend a place that he always found truly special and magical.

Rob had done the same for Jerry when years earlier he had taken him to Vinalhaven, an island about 15 miles off the coast of Maine. Rob's uncle had the lone cabin on a small mountain overlooking a northern Atlantic basin filled with seals. Jerry remembered just sitting back on that mountain while Rob played guitar, Rob's younger sister played banjo, and his Uncle Don rolled joints. That was a lot better than this.

"Remember Vinalhaven?" Jerry asked.

"Sure, not a single ghost or goblin if I recall."

After another short pause during which he remembered quite fondly some interesting adventures with local island girls and the quarry reserved for skinny dipping, Jerry said: "You're right, this is getting out of hand. Tomorrow, it's just hang out, maybe head to Charlevoix or Petoskey Beach and just have fun."

"Now, you're talking. And maybe we can just do the same for the rest of the visit. No Eddie or other craziness okay?"

Jerry nodded. "Probably best."

"Probably?"

"For sure."

"Cool." Rob put out his hand which Jerry gladly slapped with his own.

He's right, Jerry thought. *Enough is enough with all this crazy stuff.*

"Now about those women," Rob said, happy to forget about what just happened near the Shores and move on to what might be happening tomorrow. "Do you think Edina can find one for me?"

"I can call and find out."

"Now, that's what I call something worth investigating."

# # #

In Connecticut, Lucy finished her sundae and looked at her daughter. "Anne, I should have gone with Jerry to Petoskey."

"Maybe next time. Maybe someday we'll all go back there."

"Maybe we will." Lucy closed her eyes, and for a moment had that feeling, the feeling of being the most beautiful girl in the world.

# # #

When they got back to the Apple Tree, Jerry went to his room to call Edina while Rob saw the light blinking on his hotel room phone. "Shower first," Rob ignored the blink, figuring it had to be an earlier nag call from Jerry about getting ready faster. He smiled heading toward the bathroom. *Now, we can finally start having fun,* he thought.

# # #

Edina didn't seem at all surprised to hear Jerry's voice on the phone. It sounded so natural, as did hers to him the moment she answered, "Hello."

The two talked for over an hour and would have kept going a lot longer if they hadn't been interrupted by a knocking on Jerry's hotel room door.

"I better run, Edina. Can't wait for tomorrow. It just feels so great to be getting together, so right."

"Yeah," Edina said from her bedroom phone. "It does."

"We'll meet you and Lorraine at the breakwater at seven?"

"Perfect."

The 'knocking' turned into a pounding that got louder and more insistent.

"Wonderful." Jerry paused before saying "Goodnight, Edina."

Edina paused before saying, "Goodnight, Jerry," for the very first time.

Jerry smiled, as he got up to answer what had become a hammering on his door. "Coming, Rob, coming. Got really good news, man!"

When Jerry opened the door, he immediately knew that his 'really good news' had become irrelevant. As soon as he opened it, Rob said, "I have to go home. First plane out of Pellston is tomorrow morning at 6:50, I get in to Detroit at 8 or so and should be able to catch a flight to New York that would get me to the hospital by noon."

"What's wrong?" Jerry saw that all the color had drained from Rob's face.

"It's my dad," Rob whispered. "He's dying."

Chapter 11

Anne's phone rang at just after midnight. "Call from Lucy," her caller ID announced in a loud robotic voice. It made the same announcement twice more before Anne picked up the phone on the 10th ring. The last time Lucy had called so late, her dementia had her convinced that she was waking up in the house she and Harry had shared on Savannah Street in Detroit, a home not far from Hamtramck, right after the war.

"Anne," she had said that time in a panicked voice. "Help me, I can't find Daddy anywhere. Do you think he went to see Reds or Helen?"

Anne hadn't been born when Harry and Lucy first moved to Savannah Street, but in Lucy's state of mind calling her grown daughter about something that happened between her and Harry before Anne even existed made perfect sense.

The next day, when they talked about it, Lucy said that it had all just been an odd and frightening dream.

"But you weren't asleep when you called," Anne said.

"Yes, I was," Lucy insisted. "I must have been."

This time, when Anne picked up the phone, she quickly, but cautiously, said: "Mom, what's wrong?"

Anne's fears were unfounded. Lucy was perfectly lucid and in control. "I have to go to Petoskey."

#

The message to Rob on the hotel phone had been from his sister, Kelly, "Rob, Dad is in the hospital. You have to come back now. It's not good, Rob. It's not good. Call me."

"Shit." Rob quickly dialed Kelly's number, forgetting to press nine for an outside line. "Shit." He dialed again. This time Kelly answered.

"Rob, Dad called me just after dinner today and said he had such pain in his side and back that he couldn't stand it anymore. He said he could hardly breathe, Rob."

"Where did you take him? New York Presbyterian? Columbia?"

"No, Cornell. Remember that's where Doctor Makis, the oncologist works."

"Right, sorry, of course."

"Doctor Makis says he's not sure what's wrong with Dad, but with his cancer, he said it really doesn't look good."

Rob's father had been diagnosed with smoldering multiple myeloma a year and a half earlier. Lately, things had gotten worse and the word 'smoldering' was removed from the diagnosis. Multiple bone lesions in his spine caused excruciating pain and there was 'no good news' in his latest bone marrow biopsy. Still, his doctor had held out hope that the disease was treatable, giving a life expectancy of at least 2 or 3 years.

"How the hell…"

"I don't know, Rob," Kelly started to cry over the phone; her voice trembled. "Doctor Makis said he could die."

"*Could* die?"

"He said he probably *would* die and that it could be days, if not hours."

Rob's left hand, which held the phone, started to shake. He steadied it with his right and thought of his options. "I'll be there as soon as I can."

Jerry immediately offered to drive back to New York that night, but Rob had already booked his flight before heading for his friend's room.

"It's better if I fly right into LaGuardia and take a cab from the airport. What if something happened on the road, a flat tire or something? I just need to get out of here as fast as I can." Rob looked at the clock which read just past midnight.

"Maybe you can even take me to the airport now. I'll wait there until it opens and be the first in line. You'll pack my stuff up and bring it back with you in the Jeep when you come home, yeah?"

"I can drive back home tomorrow. No problem."

"No, Jer, there's nothing you can do. Just let me get there and find out what the fuck is happening. I'll call you when I know."

Jerry nodded. "Okay, man." He found his keys on the dresser. "Let's go."

# # #

"Mom, it's after midnight. Can we talk about all this tomorrow?"

"He's there you know."

"Yeah, I know Jerry's there and you wished you could have gone with him." Anne was again starting to worry about dementia.

There was a long moment of silence before Lucy answered, "Of course I know Jerry's there. That's beside the point."

"Mom, let's just get some sleep and we can discuss it all tomorrow when we're wide awake."

"I'm going."

"Mom, let's be honest, okay? You're not in the best of shape. Traveling now in your condition could be dangerous."

"Anne," Lucy voice was firm, but soft. "What can happen to me there that isn't going to happen to me here?"

# # #

The soft lights on the polished pine log carriage porch at Pellston Regional Airport created a golden glow in the deep darkness of a northern Michigan night. Jerry and Rob sat on the benches inside the outer doors to the terminal. These doors were always open to prevent a shivering winter traveler from freezing in the parking lot or a sleepy summer traveler from catching a night-time chill or getting caught in a thunderstorm.

The main doors would be opened at 5 am which gave Rob and Jerry just over 4 hours to talk, listen, and learn things they hadn't known about each other through all their years of friendship.

106

"You know my grandma on my mother's side wanted me to be a rabbi." Rob slumped back on the bench, resting his head against the vestibule wall. He laughed: "But my dad would have nothing to do with that."

"What did your dad want you to be?"

"A socialist. Anything else was gravy."

"And what about your mom?"

"A nice Jewish girl."

"So your mom was a nice Jewish girl, what did she want for you?"

"No, you don't understand, she wanted me to be a girl, a nice Jewish girl so that she would have someone to compete with."

"Oh, you're joking," Jerry smiled.

"Am I?" Rob smiled back.

"Anyway," Jerry continued. "Your mom had your younger sisters."

"True, but because I was the first, she always blamed me for wasting some of the best competitive years of her life."

"Well, my dad wanted me to join him in the bar business," Jerry laughed. "Yeah, that wouldn't have worked out too well. When I was 18, I tried to preach my version of Christianity to guys nicknamed Two Gun Eddie, Jake the Plumber (he wasn't one), and Jack the Barber (also not). Oddly enough, not one of them converted to my teenaged opinion that the Catholic Church isn't really Christian."

"Yeah, that would be kinda a tough sell."

"Hmmm," Jerry smiled at the memory. "Drunks for Jesus never did catch on."

"And your mom?"

"No real problem there, she had Anne to compete with."

Rob nodded, "Yeah, it was my mom who made us go to Hebrew school which we all hated then, but I'm kinda glad I went now."

"Why?"

"Because I can say I went to Hebrew school…in Hebrew."

"Did you guys have Bar and Bat Mitzvahs?"

"Yeah," Rob nodded. "But they were different back then. Just a bunch of people coming to the house. My dad arguing politics with Uncle Jacob in the corner, my mom holding social court in the living room bragging about my Hebrew, and the kids running around spilling stuff on their 'good clothes', and threatening anything breakable that my mom hadn't put up for its own protection."

"My folks threw First Holy Communion and Confirmation parties. Got money from my relatives, so I was cool."

"How old were you?

"Well, for the first one, around 7 and the second about 14, or so. That's how my church, Our Lady Queen of Heaven, did it. Other churches do it differently. Something about reaching the age of discretion and the age of reason."

"When did you reach those things?"

"I'll let you know when it happens."

"Gonna be a wait."

"Yeah."

"Did your family go to church a lot?" Rob asked.

"When Anne and I were little. I'll always remember the five most important words in Catholicism. "

"Hail Mary full of grace?"

"No: can we leave at Communion?"

"How'd that work?" Rob asked.

"First, you had to make sure you were sitting at the back of the church so that when everyone got up to go receive communion, you could just duck out the back door to beat the traffic. I remember once not getting into church at all."

"What happened?"

"I was going to Queen of Heaven with just my dad that day. I don't know what happened to my mom and Anne. They must have gone to an earlier mass, or maybe Anne pretended to be sick. Anyway, it just so happens that the Tigers had an early first game of a double header. So we parked on the church's street and listened to a good five innings before mass broke up, and we had to go home."

Rob laughed.

"Hey, we could see the church."

"Wasn't that like a mortal sin or something back then?"

"I asked my dad that."

"What did he say?"

"Not if the Tigers win."

Both Rob and Jerry dozed off at about 4:30 only to be awakened by the airport worker opening the inside doors.

"Morning, gents, been here long?"

"Years," Jerry said. "A lot of years."

"Thanks for waiting with me, man," Rob gave Jerry a hand shake and then a hug. "Go back to the hotel and get some rest."

"Good luck, Rob. It's going to be okay, I just really feel it is. Please let me know what's up when you can."

"Sure."

"Be strong." Jerry said.

"You too," Rob answered.

As Jerry started to walk toward the door and into the still semi darkness of early morning, he heard Rob call out, "I mean it, man, you too."

Arriving back at the Apple Tree at about 5:30, Jerry saw his phone blinking madly by his bed. It was from Anne. "Jerry, I don't know where you are, but it's after 1:30 in the morning here. Mom is driving me crazy about coming out to Petoskey. I can't bring her; I'm alone with the grandkids until Wednesday, and she keeps saying she needs to come there now. Let's all try to talk later and figure this thing out, okay? Where the hell are you? Goodnight."

"Goodnight," Jerry said hanging up the phone.

Lying down on the bed, Jerry was asleep in less than a minute. Shortly thereafter, he had a dream that he wouldn't remember for many months to come.

Chapter 12

Jerry's phone rang at 7 am. It was Anne, who had already been with their mom at her apartment for an hour.

"Good morning," he groaned into the phone.

"Where were you last night?" Anne said without the courtesy of a greeting. "I really needed to talk with you."

Jerry didn't respond to his sister's tone; instead, answering with content. "I took Rob to the airport. He's flying back to New York. His dad's in the hospital. Apparently, he's in pretty bad shape."

After a moment of silence, Anne said, "Sorry, I didn't know. Is he…"

"They don't know."

"Again, sorry. Are you okay? Can we talk now?"

"Sure," Jerry rolled out of bed. "Let me just blink a couple of times. Didn't get back here until around 5:30 or 6. I did get your message. "

"I'm with Mom. Let me put us on speaker."

"Me too," Jerry said. "I need to make a coffee while we talk."

"Can you hear us?" Anne said.

"Sure can," Jerry said. "Just a sec." He ripped open the packet of regular coffee next to the two cup pot on the counter and popped it into the coffee holder on the tiny Mr. Coffee machine. "Let me just get the water going."

"Mom," Anne said. "You wanted to talk to Jerry, so go ahead and talk."

"Maybe I should wait until after he has his coffee," Lucy half-joked. "You know how he is, and how Harry could be, before that first cup.

"Thank you, Mom. Most appreciated. But it's starting to go through so I can talk in anticipation of coffee."

"Um," Jerry heard some hesitation in his mom's voice. "Um, what's been going on up there?" Lucy asked.

Jerry thought of Eddie, the Mitchell Street Pub, the Shores, the memories. "What do you mean, Mom?"

"I don't know, Jerry. Just feeling kinda blue I guess. I just think that I should be there with you. My dreams have been so odd. They seem clear as a bell when I wake up but then they just disappear before I can even write them down."

Jerry thought of his most recent dream, hidden now just under the surface of realization. It felt like a splinter. "Yeah, I know what you mean."

"I heard Anne talking before you were on speaker phone. What is it that she is sorry she didn't know about?"

"Oh, nothing to do with me, Mom," Jerry took a sip of coffee, burning his tongue but not really giving a damn. The caffeine is what he wanted and the pain was worth it. "It's about my friend Rob. He just had to fly back to New York this morning."

"Was he getting in the way?"

"Way of what, Mom? No, his dad is in the hospital. His sister called and asked if he could come back. His dad has cancer, you know."

"Or maybe Rob just didn't belong in Petoskey."

"No, Mom. He was being great. Family emergency. That's all."

Lucy left her thought and got right to the point of the call. "Jerry, I want to come there. Is that okay, if I come there? Maybe I could even come today? It's very important that I come there. He's there."

"Who's there?"

"I mean, I mean, you're there; you're there. You know I get confused sometimes. Maybe we can find a flight today?"

Jerry could hear Anne in the background, "Mom, I told you today won't work. We have to figure all this out."

Relieved by Anne's interjection, Jerry agreed with his sister. "Yeah, Mom, today's too quick. Think Mom. It's not going to be easy for you to travel in your condition."

"You mean my condition of being just plain old?"

"You know that's not what I meant."

'Old' was exactly what Jerry meant. "Really, Mom, I'm just worried about your hip, the dizziness, everything. What if you fall down at the airport?"

"Then I fall down at the airport. Jerry, when you're this old, there's only one way to get young again."

"By traveling all the way to Petoskey."

Lucy took a deep breath. "Okay, maybe two ways."

Jerry's coffee had cooled enough for him to down the rest of the cup. "But the question, Mom, is why?"

Now Lucy smiled and very slowly and purposefully gave the answer that always drove Jerry and Anne crazy when they were kids. "Because I said so."

Both Jerry and Anne groaned, and protested, "That's not a reason."

Lucy smiled. "So, when do I come?"

"Mom, if you really want to come, maybe Anne could get you on a plane to Detroit, and I can pick you up there. Say on Sunday or Monday?"

"Why not before then? It's only Friday morning. I can come tomorrow."

Again Anne jumped in right on time as far as Jerry was concerned. "Mom, I'll need a day or two to get everything together."

Jerry's relief vanished when Anne added, "Maybe, I don't know, maybe I can get it together by tomorrow."

"No, not tomorrow!"

The intensity in Jerry's voice startled his sister, but not his mom. "Tomorrow's the 14th, isn't it?" she said. "The 14th of July." Her voice trailed off.

"Yeah," Jerry said. "I have to meet someone tomorrow."

"Eddie, right?"

"Mom, how do you know about Eddie?"

Lucy ignored Jerry's question as if it had never been asked. "Anne," Lucy turned all attention to her daughter. "Let's see about booking a flight on Sunday or Monday."

"I'll try," Anne said.

"You'll do it," Lucy corrected. "I know my girl, you will do it."

Lucy focused back on the phone call: "Jerry, does Sunday or Monday work for you to pick me up in Detroit?"

"Sure, but again how did you know about—"

"Good, Anne will let you know the flight information."

"Mom..."

"I love you more."

The connection ended with a click from the phone and Jerry's continuing question: "How did she know about Eddie?"

#

"Who is this 'Eddie' guy?" Anne asked as she started dialing Delta to check on flights to Detroit.

"Don't you worry about that," Lucy said. "Just someone your father and I knew many years ago."

#

After making a second cup of coffee, Jerry called Edina, hoping to catch her before she left for work. "Hi."

"Well, good morning." Now Edina did sound surprised to hear Jerry's voice. "What's up? Are you okay?"

Jerry told Edina all that had happened with both his mom and Rob. "Please apologize to Lorraine for both of us. I know Rob was really looking forward to meeting her."

"Oh, please don't worry. She'll totally understand. I just hope his dad is okay."

"Yeah, me too."

"Do you still want to get together today?" Edina said softly. "Or maybe you'd prefer a rain check?"

"Actually, I would very much still like to get together. Maybe more than ever if that's alright with you."

"It's more than alright. I want to as well."

"Same time as planned?" Jerry asked.

Edina looked at her watch. "You know, I have an idea. Why don't we meet at the breakwater in an hour and take it from there."

"Don't you have work?"

"Hey, I think the trout can swim along just fine without me for a day."

#

"I don't remember anyone named Eddie." Anne found her purse and fumbled for her car keys. "Was he a friend of Uncle Joe and Aunt Mary?"

# # #

Mary was Ciocia Babcia's oldest daughter. She and her husband Joe Andrews, formerly Andrzejewski, had followed her mom and sister Clara to Petoskey. They brought with them their two sons; Billy who was the same age as Anne, and Bobby who was only one month younger than Jerry. Joe died young, Mary lived to see her grandchildren. Billy became a city councilman, Bobby moved to Miami.

# # #

"No," Lucy pulled herself to her feet by the arms of the heavy high-back Victorian armchair Anne and Jerry had bought her for Christmas; getting up from the lower couch had become more and more difficult after her surgery. "Eddie was a friend to anyone who might buy him a drink or lend him money. Your father did both."

Anne started toward the door. "He sure doesn't sound like a great guy to me. But, Dad always fell for a good hard luck story."

"Eddie was okay." Lucy ignored her walker and slowly limped after her daughter and followed her out the door of her apartment. "Kind of a nut, but you're right about your dad. He sort of liked him."

Lucy grimaced from a sudden although recently familiar pain in her right knee. She paused knowing that it would be followed by a matching stabbing sensation in her left. *There it is*, she thought, closing her eyes and letting it pass.

"Mom, you don't have to walk me to the elevator. Just stay safe in your in apartment. I'm fine."

As the pains subsided, Lucy continued to follow her daughter. "That's alright, I want to see you out."

Anne shook her head. "Be careful getting back to your apartment, OK?" Anne regretted her statement before she had finished making it.

"I'm not crippled, you know," Lucy snapped. "Please, Anne, don't treat me like I can't do anything."

"Mom, I just meant—"

"I can walk my daughter to the elevator. I can still do that."

"Okay, okay, sorry, Mom." Anne pushed the down button between the two elevator doors. "I'll call you after I reach Delta. I'll try to get you there Sunday or Monday, but I don't know about tickets on such short notice."

"Anne," Lucy smiled. "If your grandma and I could put together our whole wedding in less than two weeks, I think you should be able to get one old lady an airplane ticket in a couple of days."

As the elevator door closed, Lucy turned for the slow, and once again suddenly, painful walk to her apartment. The 20 feet to her doorway seemed like a mile, but Lucy was lost in thought about another walk—one she had made many decades earlier—a walk down the aisle of St. Florian Church in Hamtramck, Michigan.

Chapter 13

"Chickens! We have to get chickens! I'll call Aunt Strina about bringing chickens!" Lucy's mom raced from room to room in their lower flat on Edwin Street. "Chickens, chickens, chickens!"

Moments earlier, seconds actually, Lucy had told her mom that Harry would be home on a ten day furlough, arriving Wednesday, May 19th. He had called her on Thursday the 13th. His first words when she answered the phone were: "Honey, I love you so much."

"Harry," Lucy closed her eyes and gripped the phone tightly. "What's wrong? Are you shipping out?"

Harry laughed: "No, I'm signing up."

"You're not volunteering for anything, Harry, are you?"

"Just one thing, Darling."

"Oh no."

"Yep, enlisting for life."

"What? But you hate the army."

"Enlisting for life with you, sweetheart. Let's get married, darling."

"Harry, you scared the bejesus out of me. We're engaged and we're going to get married, honey. As soon as we can."

"How about a week from Saturday?"

"A week from Saturday?" Lucy's eyes popped wide open. "A week from what Saturday?"

"A week from this Saturday. I should be back in town next Wednesday if the trains run on time."

Lucy dropped the phone from her right hand, catching it in her left, and returning it to her ear in time to hear Harry say that he was able to get an unexpected ten day furlough, and he wanted to get married as soon as possible.

"I want to be your hubby Harry, darling," he said. "I want that like all get-out. I hate being here without you. If we got

116

rings, then somehow, we will always be together no matter what, right?"

Lucy could hardly breathe with excitement. "Harry, I have to go."

"Why, sweetheart? Did I say something wrong? Don't you want to…"

"I have to find a dress," Lucy stammered. "Oh my God, and tell Mom!"

# # #

"Chickens, chickens, chickens!"

Lucy told her mom.

For most people, rationing and scarcities during the war made feeding a family, much less throwing a full-blown Polish wedding, a considerable challenge. But Felicia Buraczynski was going to do everything in her power to make sure her only surviving daughter's wedding day would be a memory her child would keep for life.

Lucy's mother spent the next day and a half asking, begging, and badgering relatives, friends, neighbors, and even the mailman to combine their supplies and ration books to get enough sugar, butter, and shortening to bake a wedding cake, and enough whiskey to, at the very least, half bake a hall full of wedding guests. When pleading didn't work, Felicia resorted to bartering.

Auntie Sabina immediately agreed to slaughter a dozen chickens and a like number of ducks for the occasion…in exchange for a seat at the bridal table. Several neighbors offered freshly pickled vegetables from their Victory Gardens if Felicia would provide her famous Kapusta for their Easter celebrations. Stova the butcher agreed to give a big discount on kielbasa if Mrs. Buraczynski agreed to "Never shop at that crooked good-for-nothing butcher Januk's place down the street ever again".

Januk made the same bargain in reverse.

Lucy's father, Stanley, was the Vice President of the local Knights of Columbus chapter so getting the hall wasn't a problem, as long as he agreed to invite the President, Eugene, and his crazy wife, Lottie, to the wedding.

Father Nowak was more than pleased to perform the ceremony on such short notice. "A happy blessed event is a gift from God in these troubled times."

"Tak," Felicia answered 'yes' in Polish. She crossed herself three times while thinking of where she could find the little bride and groom figures for the top of the cake.

Lucy's other best friend, Olga (the one with the 'mouth'), came to the rescue regarding the wedding dress, telling Lucy and her mom that they could use her sister Celia's wedding gown that she had been married in three years before the war.

"It's just sitting in the goddamn closet gathering dust."

"Won't Celia mind if I wear it?" Lucy asked.

"Nah," Olga sipped the cup of coffee that Lucy's mom had poured moments earlier. "Besides, she and that lousy 4F hobo husband of hers live in Scranton. Flat feet my fanny, I bet that 4fer just has a raging case of the clap or the 'chicken' shits."

"Olga, the mouth on you." Lucy turned red with embarrassment, not over what Olga had said, but the fact that she had said it in front of her mother.

"Hey, I said 'ho<u>bo</u>', didn't I?"

Olga thought of all of the windows displaying blue stars, almost every house had at least one showing their pride in having husbands or sons fighting in the war. She bit her lip when she thought of how many of those 'blue' stars turned to 'gold' almost every day. "Flat-footed coward," she whispered. "He's the one who should be dead."

"Olga." Lucy reached out and touched her friend's forearm. "Everyone's suffering in their own way."

"You're right," Olga angrily stubbed out one cigarette before calmly lighting another. She didn't want to think about what she and everyone else were always thinking about.

"He married my sister, didn't he? That's worse than anything the Japs or Heinies can dish out, right?"

Olga laughed, but it was 'War Laughter', the kind without true joy—laughter designed to cover sorrow and conceal fear. Some called it 'survivor's humor'. As one soldier said: "If I wasn't laughing, I'd be dying."

"Never mind about all that," Lucy's mom sat down at the table, waving smoke away as she spoke. "Tell me about the dress."

"Well," Olga puffed harder, she loved a stage. "It's white, as if that little sl…"

"Olga! Stop!"

"Hush," Lucy's mom told her daughter. "Did she have a veil?"

"Sure. If I had her face I'd always wear a veil."

"I don't know if this will work," Lucy said. "Celia's a little bit bigger than me."

"A little bit?" Olga stubbed and lit again. "The girl is built like a brick shithouse, but not in the good way."

Lucy weighed 102 pounds after a hearty meal. Celia had weighed in at about 185 on her wedding day, and her dress had fit like a glove.

"I'll be swimming in it," Lucy sighed. "I will look like I'm wearing curtains."

"No," Olga, ever the political one, said. "More like a tent."

Lucy's mom would have none of it. "Better too big than too small."

Over the next few minutes, Felicia gathered together her supplies. "We'll just pin it and tape it until it fits."

"Might need one of these," Olga held up the large stapler the Buraczynski's kept in their junk drawer. "It's a 'big' job. I think we need all the help we can get."

"Good thinking," Lucy's mom put the stapler, extra staples, some rubber bands, and a tube of glue into the brown bag containing the pins, both safety and straight. She also threw in tape, scotch, masking, and the new-fangled 'duct' tape Harry had brought back from his base on his last leave. "Let's get to work."

# # #

The dress was beautiful. Harry shuddered when he first saw Lucy and her father begin to walk down the long aisle at St. Florian Church that Saturday morning. Bright sunlight streaked in when the door was opened, bathing Lucy in golden glows and soft shadows.

"Am I dreaming?" he whispered to his brother Reds who stood next to him as the best man at the wedding.

"Nah," Reds whispered back. "You're an asshole."

119

Harry smiled. "Happiest asshole in the world."

"I just don't know how an ugly son of a cuss like you got so fucking lucky?"

Harry just shook his head and stared at his approaching bride.

Reds also looked at Lucy before whisper/snarling to Harry: "Love you little brother. Congratulations."

This time, Harry's smile came directly from his heart. He remembered telling Reds that first day after the candy store that he had met and would marry the most beautiful girl in the world.

Watching her slowly approach the altar, he knew she was much more than that. Harry knew he was looking at an angel: his angel.

When Lucy entered the church, she held her father's elbow tightly so she wouldn't trip or stumble. She held her breath to make sure the gown didn't come apart at the pins. She saw only Harry at the altar in his dress uniform. The people, the pews, the priest, the church itself became a blur. Lucy saw only Harry, and she knew she was looking at a hero: her hero.

# # #

Lucy could feel her father's elbow, as she gripped the balance railing that lined the hallways at the assisted living apartments. Five more steps, and she would be back in her apartment; alone with her memories, alive in her dreams, forever in love.

Chapter 14

"Blueberry muffin?" Jerry held out the bakery's brown paper bag as soon as Edina walked out onto the breakwater just over an hour after their telephone conversation. She was wearing a white sundress with a pattern of large pink and peach flowers. She looked beautiful.

Cool, Jerry, really cool, Jerry thought. *Meet up with a beautiful woman and the only thing you can say is "blueberry muffin"?*

"You know," Edina said as seductively as good taste would allow. "I don't usually muffin on a first date." She reached into the bag. "But this time, I'll make an exception."

Jerry smiled.

"Don't get your hopes up," Edina took a bite. "I'm just hungry."

Edina walked past Jerry and down the breakwater. She smiled. *Good start*, she thought. Hearing Jerry walking to catch up behind her. *Very good start.*

"That was so weird about Rob's father?" Edina said as she and Jerry walked side by side toward the end of the breakwater. "Out of nowhere?"

"It was really surprising," Jerry said. "I mean, he'd been diagnosed with multiple myeloma a while back, but he seemed to be doing OK with the treatment. I know that Rob checked before we came out here. The doctor told him that his dad probably had at least a couple of years left. Rob would never have come if his dad was in such bad shape."

"And then just boom, all of a sudden?" Edina shook her head. "And he was keeping an eye on it and everything?"

"Yeah, that's what makes it so unexpected and startling."

"Out of nowhere."

"Out of nowhere."

As they walked in silence, Jerry took a chance. He first gently brushed the outside of Edina's fingers with his. He then even more gently took the palm of her hand in his own. Edina didn't pull away.

"I'm glad you didn't go to work," Jerry said.

"Me too."

Edina and Jerry sat with their backs against the concrete light tower at the end of the breakwater until long after the seagulls gave up hope of a muffin meal. At the risk of sounding crazed, Jerry told Edina all about Eddie and the Mitchell Street Pub and all that had happened at The Hub the previous day with Rob.

With the whole story told, the two sat in silence and watched the waves until Jerry said casually as if nothing of substance had been discussed: "So what do you want to do with the day."

"I know where we should start," Edina said.

"Where?"

"Show me where The Hub used to be. That seems to be why you're here."

"I don't want you to think I'm crazy chasing ghosts or old memories."

"No," Edina said, getting up from where she sat and straightening out her dress. "It'll be fun. Show me around your childhood."

"Maybe you should leave your car at the Apple Tree," Jerry said, instantly regretting the fact that he had just inadvertently invited Edina to his hotel. *Please don't get it, please don't get it, please don't get it*, he thought, frantically hoping that his suggestion would be taken at face value alone.

She got it, but she didn't show it. "Good idea. I can drive home from there later."

Thank you, Jerry thought, expressing gratitude to either the angels that be for their cooperation, or Edina for her tact.

After the short drive from the breakwater to the Apple Tree, Edina parked her car and climbed into the Jeep. "Jerry, I was wondering about something as we drove over here. Mind if I ask you a kind of personal question?"

I was wondering some pretty personal things while we were driving too, Jerry thought, knowing that Edina's question and his continuing fantasies probably wouldn't match. "Of course, anything," he said out loud, his voice a little deeper than usual.

"Was your family really religious or spiritual? Did your parents believe in ghosts?"

Nope, not even close to a match.

# # #

When Jerry was two and half years old, Lucy's mom died. He was the only one home when it happened. Earlier, as usual, Lucy had headed off to Von Steuben elementary school where she taught third grade, and Harry had rushed to work at the paint plant.

Jerry remembered every detail of that day, including the small, bright-orange Beechcraft Bonanza single-propeller airplane with its distinctive v-shaped tail that he was playing with when his babcia told him she needed to lie on the couch and take a little rest. Within seconds, the Piaseckis' neighbor, Pani Zosia, came rushing in from the front door. It wasn't until Jerry was an adult that she told him what had happened.

Pani was in her kitchen that morning, just starting to make krupnik, Polish mushroom barley soup, for her husband's dinner. Every Monday, Pani Zosia made enough soup to last her and her husband for a week. She would always share a large bowlful with her neighbors—Lucy and Harry. Jerry loved Pani Zosia's soups, except when she made czarnina, which lists 'duck's blood' as the main ingredient.

But that Monday, she was making Jerry's favorite; krupnik so thick with barley, potatoes, mushrooms, carrots, and beef that you could stand a spoon in it and it would not fall over.

As she chopped, there was a sudden, urgent knocking on her side screen door. When Pani tried to finish cutting an onion, the pounding on the door grew louder and more insistent.

"Coming, coming, coming. Holding on to your horses," Pani Zosia said in her perfect broken English.

When she opened her side door, she saw her friend, Babcia Felicia, standing not inches away from the screen. All Felicia said was, "Come take care of Jerry."

123

It wasn't so much what Babcia Felicia had said, it wasn't even the direct and serious tone of her voice, it was the chills that raced through Pani Zosia's body that caused her to quickly tear off her apron and throw it on the floor behind her. A split second later, when she turned back to the door, Babcia Felicia was gone.

There was a vacant lot between the house where Pani Zosia and her husband, Mr. Mike, lived and the Piasecki place. It was the size of a typical Detroit lot: large enough to hold a house of say 25 feet in width, leaving enough room for a narrow driveway on one side and a three- or four-foot flower bed on the other. Pani kept the lawn on the lot manicured with her hand mower. She looked across the grass; no sign of Babcia Felicia. She looked down the driveway in case her friend had fallen, but saw only Mr. Shaeffer across the street sitting on his porch playing chess with his son Mark.

Pani almost broke her screen door, throwing it open with enough force that it loudly slammed behind her as she ran across the lawn. When she rushed into the Piasecki house, she found Felicia lifeless on the couch and Jerry playing with his little, orange Beechcraft Bonanza single-propeller airplane with its distinctive v-shaped tail.

Harry didn't believe Pani Zosia's story. "She couldn't have run back and died so fast." On that part, Pani agreed.

Lucy listened to the story. Through her tears, she knew that her mom had taken care of Jerry one last time.

# # #

"No, not a big ghost family," Jerry answered Edina's question. No point in retelling the old story that had lived, thrived, and been gloriously embellished from porch to porch in the old neighborhood until it didn't remotely resemble the event that Pani Zosia swore to her dying day was true.

Figuring all of his talk of The Hub and Eddie was more than enough for anyone to handle on a first date, Jerry reversed the question. "How about your family? Any ghost busters?"

"No," Edina laughed. "Closest we came was when my freaky cousin, Dave, decided to take LSD and claimed to have had a long talk with God about fried clams."

"That's crazy," Jerry laughed. "Now, *ribs* I would understand."

"What?"

"Nothing," Jerry put the Jeep in gear. And turned right on 31 for the ride to The Hub. "I have to save something for next time."

Edina smiled. "I look forward to next time."

# # #

Lucy used her walker when she got back into her apartment. She slowly moved to the bedroom where she sat down on the antique, carved, rosewood rocking chair, the one her mom had rocked her to sleep on as a child. The worn leather seat had been reupholstered with dark green cloth, but to Lucy, it felt the same now as it did 'then'. Putting her head back, Lucy closed her eyes and thought of her wedding night with Harry. She smiled and gently drifted off to sleep.

# # #

Jerry pulled into the Shores' parking lot. This time there was no black mass of whatever in the road and no sign of his dad. Jerry pointed to the long skid marks in the road.

"So tell me again exactly what happened yesterday," Edina said while looking at the black rubber lines and trying to read between them.

Jerry detailed the events of the previous day, although, with all that had happened in the past 24 hours, his trip with Rob to Mackinaw was a distant and increasingly indistinct memory. He had no problem recalling Rob's description of the solid black smoky thing they had hit with the car, or his imagining that he had face-to-face contact with his deceased father.

"And not a magic mushroom between you?" she asked.

"I wish," Jerry said. "At least, then there would be a rational explanation. Rob wanted me to just drop the whole thing, and to tell you the truth I was half way tempted to do just that."

"And then he had to leave."

"Yeah," Jerry said, his voice dropping off into a whisper. "Then he had to leave."

# # #

Lucy was startled from her dreams by the telephone ringing in the other room. After the second ring, the phone announced: "Call from Anne," but there was no way Lucy was going to get there in time to answer it live. After finally convincing her mom to give up her old cassette answering machine, Anne had managed, with great difficulty, to teach Lucy how to retrieve her voice mail.

"Hi Mom, it's me," Anne's voice sounded as confident and sure as always. "Just wanted to let you know that I got your tickets for Detroit. You leave on Sunday from White Plains at 12:40, getting into Metro at 2:34. I thought maybe you and Jerry could spend the night in Detroit before heading up to Petoskey on Monday."

"That would be nice," Lucy said to the voicemail message. "Then, I have you coming back on..."

Lucy hung up her phone. "I have to pack."

# # #

Jerry and Edina dangled their feet off the long white dock at the Shores. The water of Crooked Lake tickled their toes as their feet gently touched beneath the surface.

"This dock looks a lot like the one that was at the Hub," Jerry stared out at the water. "The lake looks just like I remember it."

"It's beautiful," Edina let her right leg linger a bit longer than necessary when it touched Jerry's left. "Lovely."

"Aren't they going to be annoyed that we're using their dock?" Jerry pressed his left leg ever so lightly against Edina's right.

Edina laughed. "So let them call the cops. I know all of them and their wives. Most of their kids come to the hatchery for fish camp."

"Fish camp?"

"That's what I call it."

Jerry kicked some water into the air. "You know, one other thing about this dock that I remember?"

"What's that?"

"The water is really shallow."

With that, Jerry put his arm around Edina's waist and gently pushed so that they both slid off the dock and into the water, which rose only half way up their shins. He didn't pull his arm away as they both laughed. In fact, he put his other arm around her in the pretense of preventing a fall on the slippery lake bottom.

Edina put her hands on Jerry's shoulders, as he pulled her closer in a manner both delicate and strong.

"I'm going to know you for a long time," Jerry said. They kissed. They kissed again.

"What the hell are you two doing?"

Edina and Jerry broke from their embrace, as the condo's property manager walked angrily down the dock. Suddenly, his pace slowed, and he smiled. "Edina is that you?"

"Hi, Ted." Edina waved as both she and Jerry pulled themselves back up on to the dock. "Just cooling our tootsies."

"If you say so." Ted smiled and started to turn back. "See you Tuesday for fish camp."

Edina turned to Jerry. "His, ah, kids come to fish camp."

"Got it."

"Don't let your tootsies get too cold," Ted was laughing as he left.

"Thanks Ted," Edina called out. "Best to Peg and the kids."

Jerry smiled and waved.

"Well," Edina shrugged. "I sure hope you weren't planning on keeping this a secret."

"Why's that?"

Edina pointed to the departing Ted who had already pulled out his cell phone. "Small town."

Jerry moved forward to continue what the two had started in the water.

"We better go," Edina smiled. "Again, small town."

Jerry's cell phone rang. "Maybe it's the local paper wanting a quote," Jerry joked. "We were being pretty scandalous."

"You really don't know about small town scandals, do you city boy?" Edina laughed. "We would have to do a whole bunch more than we did to make the paper around here."

"Maybe next edition?" Jerry smiled as his phone kept ringing.

"Only comes out once a week, so we have a little time." Edina pointed to Jerry's persistent telephone. "Aren't you going to get that?"

Jerry looked at his phone. "It's my sister. I better see what's up."

After a couple of minutes of saying a variety of 'okays', 'rights', 'sures', and 'yeses' Jerry said, "Goodbye".

"Everything good?" Anne asked.

"My mom's coming on Sunday," Jerry said. "I have to pick her up in Detroit."

"Want some company for the ride?"

"I'd love it," Jerry said. "But I think, I better handle this one alone."

Edina also asked if Jerry would like her to tag along to the Mitchell Street Pub on Saturday for the meeting with Eddie, but Jerry said he felt that if he didn't show up alone that Eddie might simply not be there at all.

"Well don't say I didn't offer."

Jerry put his arm around Edina, as they approached the parking lot. "Any other offers on the table."

"Only one," Edina said in semi seductive tones.

"Yes. The answer is yes!"

"Good, my offer was for you to offer to buy me dinner."

"Good offer, and I know just the place."

The Roselawn Dining Room at Stafford's Bay View Inn on Little Traverse Bay is a gentle place of white wicker, fresh flowers, crystal, and grace. It's a magical spot where chilled cherry soup and blackberry bibb salad deliciously blend into entrees such as pork schnitzel, beef tenderloin bordelaise, planked whitefish and lake perch with tomato caper relish and sherry butter sauce.

The Victorian style inn was originally built in 1886 and certainly lives up to the website claim that it has 'enchanted visitors' for almost 130 years.

"You know," Edina broke off a piece of warm bread and cut into the huge strawberry atop her salad. "As long as I've been Up North, I've always wanted to come here."

"I've been gone forever and always wanted to come back."

"To what we always wanted," Edina raised her water glass.

"To what we always wanted," Jerry lifted his glass. They clinked twice for good luck and looked into each other's eyes. They lingered in their gaze until an extremely friendly waitress asked if they were ready to order their main courses.

"Oops," Edina reached for the menu. "Forgot to look."

"No rush," the waitress smiled a genuine smile. "Here in Petoskey you have all the time in the world."

# # #

That morning in Connecticut, Lucy sang as she packed a small suitcase, *"Yes, we have no bananas, we have no bananas today."*

She couldn't remember all the lyrics to the song, but she could hear Eddie Cantor's tenor voice croon out bits and pieces of the number one song from 1923.

"We have an old fashioned to-mah-to, a Long Island Po-tah-to, but, yes, we have no bananas today."

The song always reminded Lucy of Harry.

"We sell you two kinds of red herring, dark brown and ball bearing. But, yes, we have no bananas. We have no bananas today."

Harry would belt out the song while doing his standard ukulele strum.

"Hey, Marianna, you gotta piana...we gotta no bananas today..."

But that wasn't the memory that flooded Lucy's heart, as she folded a sweater and selected a skirt. No, the image was of Harry walking into their house on Packard Street singing the song while carrying two huge bunches of bananas.

"Harry, what did you do?" Lucy had asked in shock, never having seen so many bananas in her life. "I sent you out to buy three bananas."

"They were on sale." Harry dropped the bananas on the table in the breakfast nook with a loud thud. "Ten cents a pound."

"How many did you buy?"

"Well, I had a dollar."

All totaled, the ten pounds of bananas added up to 32 pieces of fruit, all of them ripe.

All the neighbors got bananas that day, and for almost a week, the air smelled first of fried bananas and chocolate banana babka, and later, before garbage day, of just rotten bananas.

For a month, everyone referred to Harry as '*banan chlopak*', 'Banana Boy' in Polish.

Lucy thought of taking two skirts to Petoskey but knew she would only need one. *"Yes, we gotta no bananas today."*

# # #

Petoskey is known for its 'million dollar sunsets'. Legend has it that the phrase was coined at Stafford's Bay View Inn. After dinner, Edina and Jerry walked hand in hand along the bay and watched as the sun slowly dipped beneath the Lake Michigan horizon and the sky burst in an ancient gold, orange, red, and purple brilliance.

"Beautiful," Edina sighed.

Jerry had missed the sunset. He looked only at Edina. "Absolutely beautiful."

Other than Edina making Jerry promise to call her after the meeting with Eddie, "No matter how late it is", very little was said during the drive back to the Apple Tree Inn. When they got out of the Jeep, Jerry and Edina held each other and kissed in the early shadows of a young summer's night.

"Stay," Jerry whispered. "Stay with me."

Edina moved forward and said softly in Jerry's ear. "Next time."

Jerry memorized the scent of her hair. "Why next time?"

Edina pulled away and smiled. "So that we both know there will *be* a next time."

Watching Edina walk to her car, Jerry felt like a teenager entering a candy store for the very first time.

When Jerry got to his room, there was a message from Rob. By the time he had reached the hospital, his father was being released.

"They thought he was going to die for sure, Jer. They gave him only hours. My sister said they didn't even think I would make it here in time." Rob said in the voicemail. "But now the cancer's just gone. The doctors can't explain it. It's just gone."

Chapter 15

When Jerry called Rob back, both men were still trying to understand the wonderful, although, incomprehensible news.

"So he just went into remission all of a sudden? I'm no expert, but is that kind of thing even possible?"

"No, Jer," Rob said. "He didn't go into remission."

"But I thought you said…"

"The cancer is completely gone. Pain—gone, nausea—gone. Weakness—gone. The man almost broke my back giving me a hug. And speaking of backs, the doctors re-ran all the tests and even his bone lesions are just gone. The doctor told me it was like they just vanished. He's never seen anything like it."

"That's amazing."

"The doctor's Catholic. He called it a miracle. I'm Jewish, and I have to say that I agree with him.

"Mysterious ways?"

"Mysterious ways."

Before the call ended, Rob asked about the date with Edina.

"It was amazing," Jerry answered. "You're going to love her, man."

"Hmmm," Rob said. "That means you think that I'm going to meet her."

"Yeah," Jerry nodded his head. "I do believe you will."

"Well, I hope the girl has talked some sense into you and you've given up on the whole Eddie thing."

Jerry paused.

"You haven't given up on the whole Eddie thing?"

"I don't know, man. I think I'll just go there tomorrow and see what happens. Maybe he won't even show. I guess I want to see how all this craziness works out."

"*Craziness* is sure the right word for it."

"No argument there."

"You know, Jer, I almost convinced you to let go of all that weird stuff and just relax for a while. I could do it again if I was there."

And that's probably exactly why you're not here, Jerry thought.

"I can be back on the plane and be there tomorrow," Rob offered.

"No, you take care of your dad. You need to be there for him," Jerry said.

And for me, Jerry thought.

"You sure?"

"For sure." Jerry nodded his head. "Besides, I have to drive down to Detroit on Sunday to pick up my mom."

"Your mom's coming? Why?"

"Couldn't talk her out of it. She said she needs to be here."

"So what you're saying is that everyone seems to be where they need to be."

"Looks like it's lining up that way, doesn't it?"

Jerry thought he'd never be able to go to sleep that night but conked out almost as soon as he hit the pillow. He dreamed of Edina and a talking trout named Baxter.

Lucy dreamed of her hero.

Jerry didn't wake up until 9:30 the next morning, and might have slept even longer if his mom hadn't called to remind him to book her a room at the hotel in Petoskey.

"And remember, we'll be staying in Detroit for one night before heading Up North."

"I know, Mom. I already reserved two rooms at the Radisson in Farmington Hills. We can drive by our old house on Lincolnview."

"And maybe just scoot by Hamtramck and Packard?"

"We can do that on Monday morning, before heading up to Petoskey. If we get out of Detroit by noon, we should make it up here by 4 or 4:30."

"Can we drive around after you pick me up at the airport instead?" Lucy said. "I know I'll want to leave for Petoskey first thing in the morning."

"You're the boss."

"Finally you realize that."

"Trust me, Mom, I always realized that."

"Jerry," Lucy said slowly. "I really want you to know how much I appreciate this. Thank you."

"No big deal. It's fine."

"It's a very big deal to me. Maybe my most important big deal ever."

"Happy to help. I'll see you tomorrow."

Lucy paused for a moment as if she had something else she wanted to say. Jerry could hear her breathing.

"What is it, Mom?" Jerry asked.

"Um." Lucy thought better of what she was about to say. "Nothing. Nothing, Jerry. Just have a really good day today. A really, really special day today."

"Okay," Jerry said, stretching out both the 'o' and 'kay'. "But you sound weird. Is anything wrong?"

"No, absolutely nothing's wrong. Everything's right."

"Now you're sure Anne got you a wheel chair for the airport in Detroit?"

"Yes, but I really don't think I need one."

"Mom, come on, don't be silly. Why take a chance? You don't want to stumble or something before you even get out of the airport. Remember, you want to get to Petoskey in one piece right? Well, the chair will help you get what you want."

"Alright already, I'll get the chair. I just don't want to be a bother to anyone."

"But that's what the Delta people get paid to do. It's their job. So just think of it as contributing to the economy."

Lucy laughed. "Now that you put it that way, it wouldn't be patriotic of me to not have the chair."

"God bless America."

"From sea to shining sea," Lucy sang back.

"Don't sing mom, please don't sing. What if the phones are tapped? Think of those poor FBI guys and what you're putting them through."

Jerry and his mom would always kibitz about her singing, even though Jerry's tone in tunes pretty much matched hers note for note. Anne, on the other hand, had a voice that had taken her from recreation center stages in Detroit to Broadway

134

in New York. Harry always bragged that Anne's voice came from his side of the family, a boast no one could ever really seriously challenge.

"I think the FBI would much prefer my singing to hearing me complain about everything from bunions to bursitis."

"Pretty much a tossup there," Jerry laughed.

"Besides, you used to love my singing," Lucy said.

"When I was two!"

"I just don't know what happened to you after that."

"Okay, okay, okay," Jerry said. "Let's not get off the point that you will do your duty as an American and get the damn wheelchair?'

"Such language, and to your mother," Lucy teased.

"Mom, promise me you will…"

"Yes, yes, I promise. I do want to get to Petoskey in one piece."

"Great, I'll be waiting for you at baggage claim."

Lucy hesitated again before saying, "One more thing, Jerry."

"What?"

"Say hi to Eddie."

"How do you know about…"

"And Dad."

Lucy hung up, leaving her son to just look at his phone and wonder.

Jerry didn't have time to wonder for very long before his phone started beating out the reggae steel drum band sounds he had selected as his ringtone.

"Hi, it's me," Anne said when Jerry answered. "I just wanted to tell you that I did reserve a wheelchair for Mom and tried my best to convince her to use it."

"Just spoke to her," Jerry said. "She promised she would."

"You did a lot better than I did, I only got a 'probably, I'll use it'."

"Anne, did Mom tell you anything about a man named Eddie?"

"I asked her about that after our last call. All she said was that he was friend of hers and Dad's and that if you bought him a drink he'd follow you anywhere. She also said Dad had told her that he used the 's' and 'f' words a lot and that he had to keep him in line around her."

"Sounds right, but I don't know how Mom and Dad could have known him. I mean the guy looks like he could be in his early 40s, maybe even late 30s."

"Well, it probably isn't the same guy then. Maybe it's his son. You know that Mom can get things confused sometimes."

Then why the hell did she tell me to say hi to him? Jerry thought. *She also said to do the same to Dad.*

"Yeah," Jerry agreed. "It just couldn't be the same guy."

After what was starting to be an uncomfortably long moment of silence, Anne brought things down to earth. "So, what wild and crazy things are you going to do on your free day in Petoskey?"

"Well, to start, two words: cherry berry."

"Cherry berry pie at Jesperson's?" Anne almost screamed into the phone. "Now I am jealous. Mom and Dad loved that place. Are you sure it's is still there?"

"It damn well better be."

The original Jesperson's opened for business in 1903. The granddaughter of the founder invented what was to be the restaurant's most famous pie with an international reputation. One day, she was making her renowned cherry pie when she ran out of cherries half way through. A half-filled pie being a very sad thing indeed, she filled the void with raspberries—Jesperson's cherry berry pie was born.

All of Jespersen's pies were mouth-watering amazing: the other fruit varieties, the meringues, the creams. Still, it was cherry berry that starred in newspaper write-ups from the Chicago Tribune to the New York Times.

Jesperson's was yet another one of Ernest Hemingway's hangout spots when he was at the family's cabin on nearby Walloon Lake. It's said he would come in just about every day or two to have coffee and confabs with the locals, many of whom then showed up as characters in his novels.

So many places in Petoskey, those with alcohol being the most prominent and believable, claimed to be favorites of the author. Even recently opened businesses tried to cash in on the Hemingway lore. Jerry remembered passing a new shop on a downtown Petoskey Street that had a sign out front reading: *'Hemingway would have shopped here.'*

Grabbing his car keys, Jerry headed to the front desk of the Apple Tree. He wanted to be sure they had his cell number just in case anyone called, particularly Edina. He couldn't wait to dig into a slice of Jesperson's cherry berry pie. The only question that remained was whether to have it with a big scoop of vanilla ice cream or just take it straight like man.

#

"It's closed."

"What?" Jerry was shocked. "That can't be."

"It's true," the clerk at the front desk said. "Jesperson's closed."

Jerry had so happily told the clerk about his pie plans, only to have them thrown, splat, back into his face. "Closed until when?"

"Closed until forever I guess. I hear the family just got tired of running the place."

"Damn it! I was really looking forward to that pie."

"Sorry."

"What am I going to do now?"

The clerk was ready with the answer. "Well, you know there's always the strawberry pie at Big Boy's just down the street."

Jerry slapped his hands down hard on the counter and smiled. "You, my wonderful friend, are a genius."

#

The Petoskey Big Boy restaurant from Jerry's childhood featured a large dining room with a huge fiberglass statue of Big Boy in one corner. The chubby, rosy-cheeked fellow, with a big pompadour haircut, red and white checkered overalls, and holding the famous Big Boy double-decker hamburger on a tray in his right hand above his head, seemed to stare approvingly at all those consuming his edible wares.

Jerry remembered once Googling the history of the Big Boy burger during a highly intellectual and somewhat heated discussion with his sister comparing it to the Big Mac. It turned out that the 'Big Boy' was the original double-decker, with its two all-beef patties and special sauce predating the copycat-competitor McDonald's Big Mac by over 30 years.

When Jerry was younger, the Big Boy restaurant filled the southeast corner at the intersection of Rt. 131 and 31, but now that prime corner lot holds only the Golden Arches of McDonalds. The current Petoskey Big Boy is much smaller and in its third incarnation. It sits just south of Micky D's on 131 and a block or so north of the Apple Tree. Jerry headed in that direction.

Walking from parking lot to parking lot, it was only a few minutes later that Jerry found himself sitting in front of a slice of Big Boy's legendary strawberry pie with its mountain of whipped cream over whole strawberries held together by a sweet gooey strawberry filling. The pie had always been Lucy's favorite, while Harry was more of the banana cream pie persuasion. Jerry took a big fork-full of pie. It tasted like 1957.

After finishing his pie, Jerry looked at his phone for the time, still over five hours before he would meet up with Eddie. As he licked the last remnants of whipped cream from his fork, Jerry planned his day, which would include a place he often played in as a child: the Greenwood Cemetery.

Greenwood is on a cliff that decades back overlooked the old lime quarry where Jerry and his cousins would chase snakes and build rafts. Now, it's the site of the Bay Shopping Mall with not a single snake or raft in sight.

Jerry thought the cemetery would be a great place to walk off the pie and see if some of the old tombstones he and Anne used as horses were still standing. He often walked in cemeteries during his travels, feeling each tombstone told the story of a human being who laughed, cried, loved, and died. From the man who lived 100 years, to the woman who died at 23, to the baby who breathed for only a day, Jerry would carefully read every name out loud in honor of the time when those names were so often spoken in soft embracing tones, harsh inflections, or sorrowful wails.

Greenwood was founded in 1875 and serves as the final resting place for over fifteen thousand people. Jerry had only managed to walk by a small percentage of the monuments when he was stopped in his tracks by one particular headstone. He read the name three times before saying it out loud: "Edwin 'Eddie' Little. Born August 17, 1920; Died September 4, 1964 – Cpl – USMC – Purple Heart – Okinawa. May he rest in peace in the arms of the Lord."

In the wind coming in off Little Traverse Bay, Jerry could swear he heard Eddie's gravelly voice say, "Semper fucking Fi motherfucker."

Jerry got to the Mitchell Street Pub at exactly 4 pm sharp. There was no one waiting out front. He looked up the street toward the hill leading away from town to see if Eddie might be coming from around the corner by the library. The sidewalk was empty. Turning toward town, Jerry jumped back and even let out a little squeak after finding himself literally nose to nose with Eddie Little, USMC.

"Hi de ho." Eddie smiled broadly.

"Eddie!" Jerry caught his breath.

"In the flesh," the smell of whiskey and Pall Mall cigarettes swirled in the air between the two men.

"You scared the hell out of me, Eddie."

"Kinda jumpy there ain't ya, Jerry boy?"

"You always sneak up on people like that?"

"Well the Japs never seen me coming." Eddie touched his scarred and twisted leg. "Except for that one time of course."

Jerry was still too busy trying to slow his heart rate and clear his nostrils to pay much attention to Eddie's ravings about imaginary enemies from long ago wars. Still, there was that tombstone in Greenwood cemetery.

"Eddie, I want to ask you something."

"Man, you are full of questions. Let's not beat our gums standing outside of a bar. Either we go in there," he pointed to the door of the Mitchell Street Pub, "or we move out and head to The Hub."

"You do know there is no Hub, don't you? You're just bullshitting me, aren't you?"

"Did I put booze on the betting line?" Eddie laughed out loud. "Do you think I would bet booze if it wasn't a sure-as-shittin thing?"

Let's see what happens, Jerry thought. *What harm could it do?*

"Okay, let's go."

"Your jalopy nearby?" Eddie said. "I would drive, but I would do better sailing."

"Sailing?"

"Fuck yeah, Jerry boy. I'm already three sheets to the wind."

Eddie laughed at his joke, as Jerry directed him down the street. "Let's go, Eddie, Jeep's this way."

"Ain't been in a Jeep since the war," Eddie moved as fast as his limp would let him.

"It's the red one just down there," Jerry pointed half way up the block. "Closest meter I could get."

"Never heard of a red Jeep. But, what the fuck, better dead than red," Eddie said as he got into the vehicle. "Or is it better red than dead?"

Jerry started the Jeep and thought of the cemetery. "Eddie, do you know of anyone with your name being buried up at Greenwood Cemetery."

"Greenwood? What the hell were you doing at that old ghost post? Place gives me the shiver-shits, I'll tell you that right now."

"I saw a tombstone with the name Eddie Little on it."

"No," Eddie said, his voice suddenly sounding completely sober. "You saw something you didn't see."

Jerry pulled out of the parking space and headed toward The Hub. "Eddie, it was there, clear as…"

Out of the corner of his eye, it looked to Jerry as if Eddie was somehow, somehow…the only description Jerry could think of was somehow 'less than solid'.

"Eddie, you okay?"

Eddie just stared straight ahead, almost blending into the late afternoon shadows.

"Who's buried up there Eddie?" Jerry looked at the image of Eddie next to him, then back at the road.

The smell of rotting flesh filled the car.

"Woooohoooo!" Eddie shouted out, suddenly as real as ever. He waved his hand in front of his face. "Fart-fire in the hole!" Eddie laughed.

The smell almost made Jerry drive off the road. "Oh my God, Eddie!"

"One barn burner of a butt biscuit, eh Jerry boy?

"What the hell did you eat?"

"You know, I really don't remember." Eddie smiled and slapped the dashboard a dozen times as if he were playing the bongos. The stench of decomposition disappeared.

"Wait a minute, now I know what you saw, Jerry. No mystery at all about it. There is a Goddamn fucking Little buried up there at Greenwood. I forgot all about it, but everyone around this town knows the story. The guy who started up that cemetery in 1870-something-something is buried there. His name was William Little. He was a doctor in town and bought the land for a graveyard."

"That couldn't have made his patients very comfortable," Jerry chuckled.

"Yeah," Eddie said. "Good Doc Little—Full service Doctor—Birth um, treat um, and bury um."

"Quite the business plan."

"It didn't work out so good though. They say Doc Little was only 32 years old when he opened the cemetery, but that one year later, he went and kicked the bucket. Turns out he was the second one, I repeat the *second* one to be buried in Greenwood. Some other asshole died first and got the number one choice of graves. Doc Little had to settle for second best in his own graveyard. How's that for dumb fucking luck?"

"Are you related to him?"

"Hell if I know. The son of a fuck-bug never left no inheritance, so it really doesn't matter a hill of beans."

"Wait, wait, wait," Jerry shook his head. "The tombstone said the guy died in 1964, not in the 1870s."

"You must of fucked up the dates."

"No, I'm sure it said…"

"Look," Eddie snapped. "Can we just stop jawing about all this crap and get to The Hub? This boy is feeling mighty thirsty."

"Okay, okay," Jerry gave up. "I hope you won't be too disappointed, Eddie."

"I hope you won't be either."

Jerry didn't remember the rest of the ride to Crooked Lake. It was like one of those times when you're driving along and suddenly you're a dozen or so miles up the road with no memory of how you got there. All Jerry could clearly recall was Eddie singing at the top of his lungs songs like *'Heartbreak Hotel'*, *'Hot Diggity (Dog Ziggity Boom)'*, and *'Que Sera Sera Whatever Will Be Will Be.'*

It was as if no time had passed between the moment that Jerry drove out of downtown Petoskey to the second Eddie stopped singing and said: "I hope you are rolling in moolah my fine-feathered friend, because you are *buying* big time tonight."

Jerry's eyes widened, as he hit the turn signal and pulled into the grass and gravel parking lot of The Hub.

Chapter 16

Jerry stopped the Jeep just inches from one of the large boulders that marked the parking spaces in The Hub's parking lot. He skidded slightly on the small gravel stones as the Jeep came to a sudden stop. "This can't be real."

"Real is way overrated." Eddie opened the passenger side door, and despite his leg injury, jumped from the Jeep as if shot from a cannon. He leaned back in and turned his Johnson Outboard Motor hat backward, something he always did when the subject got serious. "Remember, drinks for the whole night are on you. I don't give a rat's ass about real, but a deal is a deal."

Jerry closed his eyes. *No, not real.* But, when he opened them Eddie had limped over to the driver's side door, opening it with a flourish and a bow.

"After you," he gestured with his right arm toward the front of The Hub. "Thems that doin' the buying always go first."

It's a dream. This has got to be a dream. Jerry got out of the Jeep and started walking toward the door. Eddie, a half-step behind was offering words of advice.

"Now, a couple of the rules of the road you should know about in dealing with this barkeep fella. That is if you want to stay on his good side, and you always want to stay on the very good side of the guy pouring love from a bottle."

"This isn't real," Jerry said.

Eddie wasn't listening. "Harry, did I mention his name was Harry? Ah fuck, don't matter. Anyway, Harry won't allow no fucking cussin' if a woman's even in the place. She could be in the girl's shitter, and he still won't allow it. I am telling you that the fucker can swear better than any sailor, excuse me, **Marine** I ever knew, but you put a skirt in the place, and we all have to be all polite and respectable like little altar boys on Easter fucking Sunday."

Harry?

"Second rule: when you order a whiskey, every time order a highball. That way you get a tall glass. Harry always free-pours, never uses a shot glass for measuring, so that way you always get at least a shot and a half, maybe two in the glass. But you always have to tell him to hold the ginger ale after he pours in the whiskey. That bubbly pop shit can really fuck up a highball."

Jerry actually thought of saying that whiskey and ginger ale was the definition of a highball, but he knew that Eddie was well aware of that point and simply had come up with a very practical way to get more booze for the buck.

Dream, dream, dream, only a dream.

Eddie stepped in front of Jerry and opened The Hub's door. "Welcome to my world, Jerry boy. Drinks are on you."

The Hub was just how Jerry remembered it to be, from the dark wood tables and bar in the front to the lighter, glassed-in restaurant area beyond. The smell of the place was a smell he remembered from that summer so long ago.

After four steps in, Jerry froze in both place and time. The bartender had turned to greet them with a friendly grin and nod. He held up a bottle of Kessler's and a highball glass before Eddie was half way to the bar.

"The man knows me so well."

Harry was already pouring by the time he got there.

"Enough to make a grown man cry." Eddie sat on the bar stool with a satisfied sigh.

Jerry remembered that his dad always memorized what each customer drank, and usually, had it on the bar before they managed to sit down on their regular stool.

"Harry you are a saint." Eddie slugged down his whiskey and didn't have to wait more than a ghost's heartbeat for Harry to pour another.

"Dad?" Jerry whispered. "Dad," he said louder as he started toward the bar. "Dad!"

When Jerry reached the bar, Eddie had taken off his shoe and was pounding on the bottom. Little tiny stones of coarse gray gravel fell onto the floor next to his bar stool. "Harry, you got to tell that fucking cheapskate owner that they have a new invention; they call it asphalt, maybe he's heard of it."

Eddie took off his other shoe and pounded on the heel. Again, tiny bits of gravel fell to the floor. "These stones are a pain in the ass."

"So don't put them up your ass," Harry joked and poured another half shot into Eddie's glass. "That help your aching feet?"

"Well, I certainly ain't complaining," Eddie's eyes grew wide, and he licked his lips. "Not any more anyway."

"Who you drinking with today?" Harry asked looking from Eddie to Jerry and back again.

Eddie made the introduction. "Harry, this is my new drinking, and paying, buddy Jerry. Jerry, meet Harry. Harry meet Jerry. Okay let's drink. Oh and pass the beer nuts will ya? It feels like I ain't eaten anything in forever."

Speaking now through a mouthful of beer nuts, Eddie kept talking. "And have the cook throw on a few Hub burgers for the three of us. We can have a real lady-like late lunch. After all, Jerry-boy's paying, so lunch is on him."

"That copacetic with you?" Harry asked the man named Jerry to whom he had just been introduced.

"Sure, sure," Jerry was almost in shock. *Having hamburgers with my dad, my dead dad,* he thought. *Just a dream.*

"Hey, Carl," Harry called out to the waiter who was standing near the kitchen. "Could you tell Frank to slap on three burgers?"

"And fries," Eddie said. "Don't forget the fries."

"And fries," Harry called out.

"Fuck if I know why." Eddie rubbed his belly. "But it seems like food just goes right through me these days."

Jerry's last memory of his dad was of a man with stooped shoulders and a sad expression of acceptance of his fate and the inevitability of his fast approaching death. Jerry remembered how a few months before his final stroke, his dad had turned to him and said, "I already told your sister and I want to tell you too: son, take care of your mother."

"Dad, you'll be here to take care of her yourself for a long, long time."

Harry had smiled a little smile of gratitude before saying without emotion, "No, son. I'm shot."

They were words that were always close to the surface of Jerry's thoughts and never left his heart.

The man behind the bar was Harry Piasecki as a young man, perhaps, 35 or maybe 37 years old. He wore his customary bartending outfit—white shirt, bright color tie with a race horse tie clip, and long white apron tied at the waist. He was thin enough in those days that the apron string circled his body twice before being tied in the back.

Harry's stomach was flat, his shoulders were strong, his smile vibrant, and his gray-blue eyes sparkled with the anticipation and dreams known only by the young. His brown hair had only just started to recede on either side of a wavy middle-top front tuft; something Jerry later would call his 'dock'.

"I have a son named Jerry," Harry said holding out his hand.

Jerry felt his father's strong, rough, and weathered hands for the first time since his final visit to the nursing home where he had died decades earlier.

"Name's Harry, Harry Piasecki."

Jerry remembered how his father had taught him to have a firm handshake when he was five years old. He had never forgotten what his dad's hand felt like squeezing his just enough to make a point, but not enough to hurt. Now, Jerry squeezed back with just the right amount of pressure, just as he'd been taught.

"Jerry," Jerry said while looking deeply into his father's eyes. "Jerry Piasecki."

# # #

Lucy felt a sudden and profound chill that quickly turned into the gentle warmth of a loving embrace. She had just sat down to have a fried baloney and sautéed onions on rye bread sandwich; just like the one she invented for Harry when they were first married. The feeling swept over and through her as she was about to take her first bite. It hit like a gale before dissolving into a soft breeze.

Getting up from the table, she slowly made her way to her closet where she kept important papers and memories in a long, green, metal tackle box. She rummaged past her birth and baptismal certificates, faded old black and white wallet sized photographs of her children and her wedding, Christmas greetings from people now long gone, and Harry's funeral card which read, *'Beloved Husband of Lucille, Always.'* Finally Lucy found what she was looking for: her half of a torn 1940 dollar bill. It was a piece of crinkled paper that would forever connect her with her love.

Finding her purse on the coffee table in the living room, Lucy gently kissed the bill, and read the top line *'SILVER CERTIF...'* where Harry had torn the dollar in half, keeping the half that included the *'ICATE'* part of the banner wording.

"Imagine, Harry," Lucy said out loud. "A silver certificate. They sure don't make them like that anymore, do they, honey?"

In her mind, she could see Harry put his half of the bill in his pants pocket before leaning over to kiss her in the light of the setting sun.

"I might be needing this." Lucy put her half of the dollar into the zipper compartment of her wallet. It was where she had kept Harry's last driver's license since the day he passed away. Wallets changed, but where Lucy kept the driver's license never did. She put the wallet back in her purse.

Smiling, Lucy slowly returned to her fried baloney sandwich which she cut in half to save for later.

# # #

Harry yanked his hand away. "Stop pulling my leg." He turned to Eddie, "What kind of bullshit setup is this?"

Eddie just shrugged and pushed his empty glass toward Harry.

Harry poured whiskey into Eddie's glass but looked at him with a no nonsense stare. "You know better than to bring my family into some kind of joke."

"No joke." Eddie put his hands up in the air. "I just met this guy the other night in town. Seemed like a crazy motherfucker, but an offer to buy for the night is an offer to buy for the night."

"What do you mean crazy?" Harry asked."

"Bat shit loco loony wack-job," Eddie laughed. "He said The Hub wasn't here anymore; that it had been replaced by a bunch of rubbers."

"Condominiums," Jerry corrected.

"See," Eddie said. "You ain't in The Hub no more Harry but inside some condom made by a company named Iniums."

He drank his second drink and finished his first beer. "I'm a Trojan man myself." Eddie belched. "Hey Harry, remember the slogan the army passed out in the war: 'Put it on before you put it in'? We'll, I say put it in and fuck it."

"Eddie," Harry said, "I swear to God if you two are in cahoots about…"

"No one is in cahoots about anything." Jerry sat down on a bar stool next to Eddie. He pulled out his New York driver's license. "See?"

Harry hesitated before looking at the odd and brightly colored license with a photograph of the man sitting in front of him. It said it was a driver's license, and it was issued to 'Jerome Piasecki'.

The thing was clearly a fake as it sure didn't look like any driver's license Harry had ever seen, and he had carded thousands of under-aged fellas who had tried to sneak in for a drink or two. Still, Harry stared at the name on the front: 'Jerome Piasecki'.

"How did you know Jerry's real name is Jerome?"

"I didn't know that," Eddie called out. "Why would you saddle a kid with a name like Jerome? Must have gotten the piss teased out of him at school."

"Shut up, Eddie." Harry turned to Jerry. "You better not be pulling my leg. Who the hell are you?"

"I'm your son."

Harry was about to punch this asshole in the face.

"I can prove it."

"You got ten seconds before I throw you out on your ass."

"Oh, if he does throw you out," Eddie quickly interjected, "leave enough money for my tab. A bet's a bet buddy boy."

Jerry blurted out the first memory he could think of; "Gillette Friday night fights."

"What about them?" Harry asked. "They're still on."

Jerry forgot which year the Gillette Cavalcade of Sports boxing matches from Madison Square Garden went off the air, but it didn't really matter to the story. "You used to watch them with Grandma, remember?"

Back before Lucy's mom died, she and Harry would have good natured competitions as to whether to watch boxing, as Harry wanted, or professional wrestling, which Babcia Felicia just loved. They were both on at the same time on Friday night.

"Boks." Harry would say the word boxing in Polish every Friday evening as he turned on the TV.

"*Nie, zapasy,*" his mother-in-law would call for wrestling.

"*Boks.*"

"*Zapasy.*"

"*Boks.*"

"*Zapasy.*"

"*Boks.*"

Every week, Lucy would intervene and, with a wink, plead with her mother to let Harry watch boxing. "He works so hard, Mama," Lucy would try not to laugh. "Just this week, please let the man watch his boxing."

Finally, each week, Lucy's mom would reluctantly agree, hiding a smile under fake indignation over having to give in.

At that point, Harry would hit the couch and focus on the televised boxing match. His mother-in-law would sit in a brown overstuffed easy chair with white doilies on its arms and focus on Harry.

Usually within five minutes, ten at the most, Harry would be sound asleep on the couch. As soon as she heard snoring, Lucy's mom would quietly get up and tiptoe to the TV set and switch the channel to wrestling.

"I'm not asleep," Harry would snort out from under a snore, which caused Lucy's mom to switch back to boxing. Now, she didn't bother to sit down, but stayed by the TV until the snoring returned. Generally after the second "I'm not asleep", Harry would be zonked for at least an hour, often two.

Lucy's mom loved wrestling and would argue at the top of her Polish lungs that it was real. Her favorite wrestlers were

Gorgeous George, the Sheik of Araby and, above all others, Crusher Lisowski, who Lucy called her mother's Polish blond bombshell. Her mom would wave her hand to dismiss her daughter's comments while secretly admitting to herself that she found the 'Crusher' to be awfully cute. *I wonder what part of Poland his family is from?*

Usually, Lucy would curl up on the floor next to her mother's knees and watch wrestling with her, always laughing at her mom's silent enthusiasm for the so-called sport. Sometimes, little Anne would come into the room and in the sweetest voice a five-year-old could muster request a quick channel change to roller derby.

"Can I watch Toughie Brasuhn?" Anne would ask to see her favorite roller derby queen demolish the competition, even though the star skater for the Brooklyn Red Devils was all of 4 foot 11, weighing in at 135 pounds.

Lucy and her mom would always agree, partially, because they wanted to be nice to Anne, and mostly because they enjoyed watching Toughie's husband, and matinee idol, Ken Monte, the 'Terror on Eight Wheels' skate for the men's team.

Once the roller derby and wrestling were over, Lucy would turn off the TV which invariably caused Harry to jerk upright and awake. "What happened in the fight?" he would ask.

Lucy would run her hand through her husband's hair. "Honey, you were knocked out cold."

# # #

"How did you know that story?" Harry leaned over the bar toward the man sitting next to Eddie.

"Mom told me," Jerry said.

"Mom?"

"Lucy."

Harry pulled away. "Bullshit. Get the fuck out of my bar, or I swear to God I'm going to belt you one where you sit. You don't mention Lucy ever. No one mentions Lucy ever."

"Not even her son?" Jerry got up and started walking toward the door as he asked his question, which he knew was a wise and prudent thing to do under the circumstances. "A son you wanted to name Tommy."

Harry jumped up butt first on the bar and spun around so that he could jump down and run after the man claiming to be a grown-up version of his son. "Nobody knows about Tommy. Nobody."

"Dad," Jerry turned and again looked deeply into his father's eyes as he never dreamed of doing as a kid. It was something he had always regretted. "I am telling you the truth. As God is my witness, I am."

"Sit down," Harry motioned to the nearest table. "You've got five minutes to tell me more."

As Carl brought out the burgers and fries, Jerry went through family story after family story, making sure that none of them happened after his seventh birthday, which was still two weeks into the future for Harry. He told his dad about how before the war he almost joined the Washington Senators baseball farm system but had to give up on baseball to care for his sick mother.

"You were too short for football in high school, so you ran track. Your red hair turned brown and you grew six inches after you graduated."

Jerry tried to think of the smallest details of everyday life, things only a family member would know. He talked about how his dad would brag that he only used two teaspoons worth of sugar in his coffee. While technically true, Harry had an unusual way of counting to two. He would hold the glass sugar pourer upside down and pouring into his cup while he leisurely stirred in the first spoonful, and while he slowly brought the spoon back up to measure the second. He kept pouring until the stirring was done. Harry always stirred his coffee exactly 25 times.

Harry stared at Jerry closely the whole time he was talking. "You don't really look like Jerry."

"The last time you saw me I was just going on seven years old."

"That was this morning."

"To you it was this morning. To me it was a long time ago."

Harry shook his head, "You know this is all nuts, right?"

"Actually, Dad, I agree with you there. This is all nuts. Totally nuts. I have no idea how any of this can be happening, but it is. Maybe I'm just dreaming. Maybe you're not real at all. That's the only thing I can think of. Either you're just part of some crazy dream I'm having or maybe I'm some crazy part of yours."

"Does this feel like a dream?" Harry took Jerry's hand and put it against his cheek. "Pretty damn real, right?"

"Oh my God," Jerry whispered as he felt his dad's stubbly whiskers that had seemed so rough and wonderful to him as a kid. He suddenly thought of sliding down his father's shin from knee to toes over crossed legs. "It is you."

"Okay," Harry quickly let go of Jerry's hand. "Before you start bawling…"

Actually it was Harry who reigned in his emotions. There was something when he put the back of this man's hand against his face that felt so familiar and fine.

"Dad." Jerry whispered.

Harry thought the word *son*, but quickly pushed that thought away. "Let's say that, just for a second, I believe you, which I don't. But let's say that I did, again I don't, then I would ask you about what happens."

"What happens when?"

"In the future."

Jerry shook his head. "Dad, I don't think I should talk about that. We don't know, it might change things."

"You have to give me something."

Jerry took a deep breath. "Okay, I can tell you that you and Mom love each other, I mean really love each other, for the rest of your lives."

Harry very slowly pushed his chair back and got up from the table. "That's all I've really got to know."

Jerry and Harry, son and father, firmly shook hands through time and space, past and present, earth and spirit. "I love you, Dad."

"You know I still think you're full of shit?" Harry smiled.

"I know you do."

"I sure as hell am never going to tell you about this crazy stuff."

"I know you won't, because you didn't."

"But if there's any way even a word of what you said is true. Come back when I'm in my 80s, and we'll talk it over then."

Jerry couldn't tell his dad that he died of multiple strokes when he was 56 and that at this point he had already been dead for almost 30 years.

"Okay, Dad, will do."

Before they could say another word, four fisherman walked in and took up seats at the bar to Eddie's right. Then two young women, both wearing sleeveless sundresses with matching pumps on their feet, sat on stools to Eddie's left.

Glancing at the women, Eddie raised his hand up in the air and called out, "I know, I know, Harry: no cussing."

"Gotta work," Harry said, walking back toward his post behind the bar. "I still don't believe your cockamamie story."

"That's okay." Jerry followed his father to the bar. "Dad."

Harry looked at Jerry, gave a barely noticeable nod, and started pouring his customers' favorite drinks.

Jerry left Eddie at the bar with half his burger, most of his fries and two 20-dollar bills. "That good for the night?" Jerry asked.

"Hell, with forty bucks I'm good for about forever," Eddie laughed. He crossed himself, "Eternal drinking here I come."

Without looking back, Jerry walked quickly out of The Hub and directly into the arms of a waiting state trooper.

"Sir," the trooper stepped back from Jerry, whose eyes were just starting to adjust to the early evening light. "Is that your Jeep?" the trooper stepped, pointing to a red Jeep that was parked right up against a pedestal holding a stone slab with the words: *'The Shores'* neatly engraved on both sides.

Chapter 17

After apologizing for crushing a fern in front of the sign, promising to pay for any damages and passing a sobriety test, Jerry drove indirectly back to the Apple Tree. One stop was at a liquor store; Jerry desperately wanted a drink. No, Jerry desperately wanted to get drunk. He pulled over three other times so that he could stop shaking long enough to keep the car from jitterbugging all over the road.

Once in his room, he poured himself a straight Scotch, envisioning his father free-pouring a drink for Eddie.

"It all had to be a dream."

Jerry took off his shoes and watched as a dozen or so tiny stones of coarse, gray gravel fell onto the floor of his room. Jerry stared down at the stones for more than a minute before suddenly jumping up and almost running to the sink. Wetting a paper towel, he raced back to where the gravel had fallen and furiously cleaned up the remnants of the parking lot at The Hub. He wanted the floor to appear as if the gravel was never really there.

"I am going nuts," Jerry said out loud. "Get it together asshole. You're going to end up in a psych ward if you keep this up."

As if in response to its own madness, Jerry's mind diverted itself from the mystifying to something magical and more manageable. *Edina, I promised to call Edina*, Jerry thought. *Get real. Get real. Get real. Get real. Get real.*

After talking to Edina, Jerry felt much more in control. He didn't need to go over the specifics of what had happened that day. He simply wanted someone to help him hold on to his sanity and self. Edina had been happy to listen and say very little—exactly what Jerry needed.

Picking up the bottle of Scotch, Jerry looked down at the floor one last time before grabbing his glass and heading out onto the balcony. Once there, he sat and toasted to the blinking light tower in Harbor Springs which alternately lit up the bay with its eerie green light before returning it to perfect blackness and all the secrets kept hidden in the night.

Funny, Jerry thought. *It's like the green light shows you something and then takes it away. Just like everything else around here. Fuck it.*

"*Na zdrowie,*" Jerry raised his glass. "*Na zdrowie.*" He drank.

After the third toast to the light and the darkness, Jerry wondered why in Polish '*na zdrowie*' is used as 'to your health' when drinking and as 'God bless you' after someone sneezes. After the fourth toast, he stopped thinking about it.

Jerry didn't remember setting the alarm or ordering the wakeup call that came moments after he was jolted awake by the sound of marimba music blasting happily from his telephone at seven the next morning. In fact, he had no idea how he got to bed at all, remembering only sitting on the balcony and being mesmerized by the green light streaking over the water.

The half empty bottle of Scotch on the dresser explained it all, except for a dream Jerry suddenly remembered as he sat up in bed. It wasn't really a dream so much as a voice he heard in his sleep just before the alarm sounded. It was his father's voice telling him; "Wake up, Jerry. Time to bring Mother to me."

"I know, Dad. I know," Jerry said out loud. "Crazy dream. Crazy, crazy dreams."

Still, Jerry had to admit that it was time to get moving. He wanted to be on the road by 9 to give him plenty of time to arrive early at Detroit Metro Airport, park the car and get inside to meet his mom at luggage.

He again imagined hearing his father's voice. "Alright, Dad, I'm up! I'll bring her!"

Now you're talking to voices in your head; instructions from a dead man. Yeeaaaahhhhh.

A few cups of strong coffee, a couple of extra strength Motrins and a long, long shower got rid of the pounding in Jerry's head and the cobwebs cluttering his brain. By quarter to nine, he was in the Jeep turning left onto U.S. 131 South for the four, maybe four and half hour drive to Detroit.

"Going Dad! Coming Mom!" he shouted out in order to preempt any voices that might see fit to nudge him on his way.

# # #

Anne and Lucy got to Westchester County Airport three hours before the flight. Lucy had insisted on the early arrival, "Just in case."

Westchester is a small airport about seven minutes outside of White Plains, New York. With the parking garage just across the airport access road from the terminal, and easy curbside drop off and pick-up, it beat the hell out of trying to get to Kennedy or LaGuardia. There you end up walking what seems like miles through throngs of other travelers and often waiting endlessly for flights delayed by either mechanical issues or crews caught in traffic.

"I don't think I need a wheelchair here," Lucy said as they pulled up right in front of the terminal door. Still, one was waiting for her as arranged by Anne, supported by Jerry and insisted upon by both.

"I'll be right back," Anne told the Delta attendant behind the chair. "Let me just park the car."

Even though the parking structure was only 50 or so feet away, a Westchester County police officer told Anne she could just pull over past the entryway and park there while she saw her mother off.

It took only a few minutes to check Lucy's bag and walker at the counter. Anne had printed up her mom's boarding pass the night before. Lucy and Ann hugged as they got to security. "I love you, Mom."

"More," Lucy said as the attendant pushed her down the empty aisle and through the doors to the glass enclosed security check points and body scanners.

Anne watched from the other side of the glass, as her mom told the attendant to stop for a moment, just long enough for her to blow her daughter a kiss goodbye.

#

Jerry arrived at Detroit Metropolitan Airport an hour early. Lucy's plane was right on time. When his iPhone rang, announcing a call from 'Lucy P', Jerry was already waiting at baggage claim.

"Mom, you're here!" Jerry smiled as he hit accept.

"We are on the way to luggage," Lucy sounded genuinely happy and unusually excited. "Can't wait to see you!"

"You do have a chair right?"

"Yep, they were waiting for me right at the gate. All this service, I feel like the Queen of Sheba."

"Well, your humble servant-son and your next carriage await."

"I should hope so," Lucy tried to sound regal. "After all, I am a queen."

Fortunately for Jerry's back, this queen traveled light. They waited only five minutes or so before her carry-on suitcase, which she had checked, and her foldable walker arrived on luggage belt 3.

"Where are you parked?" the Delta worker who had pushed the wheelchair from the gate asked.

"Short term lot, really pretty close."

"Come on," the young man said. "I'll wheel her there for you."

"Thank you," Lucy smiled up at the man.

"That would be so great," Jerry said. "Can I pay you?"

"Nah," the young man smiled a grin so genuine that it would remain a photograph in Jerry's memory. "How often do I get to push around the Queen of Sheba."

Random acts of kindness, Jerry thought of the phrase and of how applicable it was all over the world, but somehow even more so in Detroit. Maybe he felt that way because it was where he grew up. Maybe it was just this helpful young man. Maybe it was because when people struggle they often must struggle together.

Or maybe because it's true. Jerry put the thoughts aside as they got to the car, "All set?"

"You bet," Lucy responded. "Ready-o?"

"Let's go!"

Jerry pulled the car out of the parking space and began a journey with his mom that would take him to the edge of sanity and the beginning of eternity.

"Like I told you, I reserved two rooms at the Radisson in Farmington Hills," Jerry said while exiting the lot. "Want to go there and get some rest? You must be tired."

"Not at all," Lucy said. "I'll have plenty of time to rest soon. I want to go to Hamtramck."

"Now?"

"Do you mind driving around for a little while? You know, I haven't seen the old neighborhood in years."

"Sure." Jerry took the entrance onto Interstate 94 east toward Detroit, instead of going west toward Farmington Hills. In Detroit many people, particularly those living on the east side, call the road the Edsel Ford Freeway, or just 'the Ford.'

"Honestly," Jerry had a sudden burst of energy and something he could only describe as *happiness*, "I'm really happy to do it."

Hamtramck, Michigan covers only about 2 square miles, but Jerry and Lucy drove from street to street for over an hour and a half. Lucy was mostly silent, staring out at what is Hamtramck today *and what it was*, she thought, *when it was mine.*

Lucy had Jerry stop in front of what had been the site of her father's candy store. She could hear the bell ding-a-ling when someone opened the shop door and pulled its chain. She remembered the one time when she looked up after the ding-a-ling to see Harry for the first time.

Now, all that remained was a vacant lot between familiar old houses where Lucy as a child would visit neighbors and play 'grownup' with friends.

"That's where my father's store was," she pointed to the abandoned space now overgrown with weeds. In her mind, she could still see the wording on the windows: *'Candy – 1 Cent'*, *'Beer – TAKE OUT'*, and *'ICE CREAM DIPS – 5 cents'*.

Lucy stared above the vacant lot at about the level where the second floor flat she grew up in once existed. She had spent most of her young life in that upper flat. That was before her parents moved to Edwin Street just before the war.

"Let's go," Lucy sighed.

"Mom, what's wrong? It's just a vacant lot."

"Not to me. Let's go."

A few minutes later, driving down Joseph Campau Street, Lucy saw the store where her mom bought live fish from an old wooden barrel and live chickens to keep in the basement until Sunday. The actual store was long gone, but the memory stayed vivid and real.

"We used to get fresh pickles there," Lucy pointed to another vacant lot. "And right there was the butcher shop where your grandmother picketed with the other women over price increases."

"When was that?" Jerry asked.

"Oh that was during the Depression. Your grandma was quite the rebel. She led the other women in the protest over price gouging and whenever a man would come out of the butcher shop with meat she would grab it, rip off the paper, and throw it in the dirt."

"Go Grandma!"

"I saw her do it once to a man who was twice her size. She made him run away down the street."

"You must have been so proud of her."

"Are you kidding?" Lucy smiled. "I was a young teenager. I was sooooo embarrassed. I didn't want to go to school for a week."

A little farther down the road, Lucy pointed to what had been Federals Department Store, Cunningham Drug Store, and finally, Sweetland—where she and Wanda, and later she and Harry would share giant sundaes and talk about even bigger dreams.

"We can go to the hotel now," Lucy said softly, looking at the present as being almost blasphemous to the past. It all made her angry and very sad.

"Want to drive by Packard?"

"No," Lucy said, deciding to always remember their home on Packard as it was, not as the way it might be today. *What if they tore it down?* Lucy couldn't bear the thought. "I am getting tired. I've seen enough for today. "

"No problem, Mom," Jerry turned right on Caniff and headed toward Interstate 75 which cut through part of the far western section of Hamtramck where Harry grew up. So many houses were leveled to build the expressway, but Harry's house on Nagel Street was on the edge of the destruction back then and still stands today.

Lucy looked to her right as Jerry drove north.

"Isn't that where Dad grew up?" Jerry asked pointing to the 900-square-foot, single-story home that someone had covered with light beige aluminum and cheap faux brick siding somewhere in the early 1960s. The two bedroom, one bathroom house was the home of the Piaseckis: Harry, his mother, father, four sisters, two brothers, and the memory of the two others who died there.

"I can't believe it's still standing," Lucy said. She thought of all that her Harry had endured growing up behind those walls: his father's strap, his mother's drunken screams, his dying siblings, and the real and biting hunger of the times.

After he and Lucy were married, Harry only stepped foot in the house three times. Once to get his belongings, once when his mother died from drink shortly after the war, and one final time when his dad died a year later. Anne and Jerry never met their paternal grandparents. Both were dead and memories of them buried before the kids were born. What they knew came from Lucy; Harry never spoke of them at all.

"They should have torn it down long ago," Lucy looked away from the house and straight ahead down the freeway. "Drive faster."

"What's the rush?"

"I don't know. Just seeing this place like it is today makes my life seem like a ghost from the past. Some things are the same, like St. Florian's, but most everything else, including where I grew up, is gone."

"There's still Three Star," Jerry offered, having been more than a bit excited when they drove by Three Star Barbecue on Joseph Campau and Commor. There had also been a Three Star restaurant a bit farther south on the same side of the block, but that was gone.

"Yes, but that's pretty much it."

"I guess time changes everything for everyone, right? Where you grew up is never the same."

"Or, it's always the same," Lucy said. "That's the way I want to think about it anyway."

The Jeep zoomed past East McNichols (6 Mile Rd. to East Siders), then 7 Mile road, and finally, 8 before Jerry broke the silence. "I hope you're okay with Petoskey. You know a lot has changed up there too."

"No, it will be fine. You'll take me to The Hub."

"But, Mom, I told you that The Hub is now a condo complex called 'The Shores'."

Lucy just stared out the window and whispered under her breath, "You'll take me to The Hub."

"Mom, I'm sorry. Maybe it was a mistake to drive through Hamtramck."

"No, no, no, honey," Lucy smiled. "It was really good to see the old neighborhood. I needed to say goodbye."

Lucy wanted to go right to her room when they got to the hotel in Farmington Hills. Jerry had, of course, suggested ribs at the Bone Yard.

"I wish we had stopped at Three Star, but the Bone Yard will do."

"No, you go, sweetie. It's been a long day."

"You gotta eat."

"I'm not really hungry."

"Are you sure?"

"Positive."

"Maybe I can bring you back…"

"Honey, I AM REALLY NOT HUNGRY," Lucy snapped out the words in that mom's voice that every child knows means she or he is really getting on their mother's nerves. Ribs made Lucy think of dancing with Harry in the kitchen just before sunrise. She knew having them would make her cry. She didn't want to cry. She felt like she no longer needed to cry.

"Got ya, Mom. I guess I should just be…"

"Going? Yes. Please. I love you. Go!"

After walking Lucy to her room, Jerry stood in the hallway just outside the suite. "Is there anything you need?"

"Are you still here?" Lucy closed and double locked the door.

As Jerry happily ordered his ribs at the Bone Yard, he thought of his dad and his dad's family all living in a house no bigger than a small apartment. As adults, all of his aunts and uncles, as well as his dad had put on a few…a lot…of pounds, and Jerry wondered if they could all even fit in the house if they were alive today.

As the ribs were about to arrive, Jerry worked to put any thought of weight out of his mind. *I'll diet tomorrow, or soon at the very latest.*

Harry and his six siblings never dieted; something one tends not to do after almost dying of hunger. Nobody became rich as adults, but there was enough money to buy food, which was something none of the family scrimped on. When a meal was served, it was always plentiful, and most of all, appreciated deeply by each member of the family.

Jerry remembered one day when he was working at the bar in Detroit during college, well after that summer at The Hub, when one fairly inebriated customer started teasing his dad about his weight, "Harry, you are really packing on the pounds."

Jerry worried that his dad was going to get angry, but instead, he had grinned a big grin and patted his now bulging belly with both hands. "And I earned every pound."

In her hotel room, Lucy took the torn dollar bill from her wallet and placed it under her pillow.

At 3 that morning, Jerry heard a knocking on his hotel room door. On opening it, he saw his mom standing in her white cotton nightgown and light pink nylon robe. She had one hand on her walker as the other prepared to knock once more when Jerry flipped free the chain lock and turned the deadbolt.

"Mom, what's wrong?" Jerry moved to the side so his mom could step into the room.

Instead, she stood still in the hallway. Looking up at her son Lucy said. "Did you see Dad? Did you see him? Tell me the truth."

"Mom," Jerry said. "I think you better come in."

Chapter 18

Now there's a question, Jerry thought while holding the door open for Lucy to come into his room. *When your mom asks you if you saw your dead father, what are you supposed to say: 'Sure, yesterday, we had lunch?' This is all too crazy.*

Lucy moved slowly across the room and sat on the edge of the bed. "So are you going to tell me or not?"

Jerry decided to avoid answering his mom's question by asking one of his own. "What do you mean, Mom? How could I have seen Dad? He's been gone so long."

"You met with Eddie yesterday, right?"

"He's just some wacko drunk guy I met at the Mitchell Street Pub."

"Hmmm," Lucy said softly, but in a way that meant that Eddie was much more than a drunken wacko.

"What do you mean by 'hmmm', Mom? The guy is…"

"Did he take you to The Hub? Did you talk with Dad?"

Jerry let out a deep breath. "Mom, to be honest, I don't know what happened yesterday, I really don't. I do know that I almost got arrested for crushing a plant at the Shores Condominiums, which are where The Hub used to be."

"You did talk to him didn't you?" Lucy smiled before getting up to leave. Holding on to her walker, she moved more quickly than Jerry thought possible.

"Mom, don't go. Everything is so mixed up."

"No it's not, Jerry." Lucy reached and opened the door. "You don't have to tell me about it, but now I know that you did see him and that you did talk to him. And you know what? That's all I've really got to know. "

That's just what Dad said.

As Lucy left, Jerry followed her into the hallway. "How do you know that I saw Dad?"

Lucy kept moving toward her room. She didn't turn around when she said; "Because when you were almost seven-years-old, Dad told me so."

That night Jerry dreamed that he was working in the bar with his father, not The Hub on Crooked Lake but the 7 Mile Hub in Detroit. There was really nothing extraordinary in the dream at all, just a normal day at the bar. Patsy Cline's song *'Crazy'* played softly on the jukebox, and a Tigers/Yankees game flickered forth from the 25-inch Zenith color TV that Harry had mounted just below the ceiling at the front of the bar.

Men clapped and cheered for Al Kaline, Willie Horton, or Norm Cash and booed and cussed when Mickey Mantle, Joe Pepitone, or particularly, Rocky Colavito—a former Detroit Tiger—came to bat.

Seven men sat in three groups along the bar. All of them worked on the line at either Dodge Main, Ford's or one of the other plants in the neighborhood. Harry Piasecki was shooting the bull with Hobart and Foxy at one end of the bar, while Jerry poured drinks, free style like his father, at the other.

When the telephone rang from the back room, all seven men immediately shouted out: "I'm not here," as Jerry went to answer the call.

It had been one of the first lessons his father had taught him about running a bar: when the telephone rang, it was most likely a wife trying to track down an errant hubby. So the protocol was to say, "Let me look." (Pause) "No, not here, don't see him."

If in fact the man being sought was, indeed, at the bar, the fellow in question was to be told immediately so that he could slug down his drink, slug down another, and get the hell out of there lest his woman decide to see for herself whether her dearly beloved was just out for a walk as she had been told...several hours earlier.

One time Foxy drank a bit too slowly after being told that it had been his wife, Doris, on the line. His good buddy, Max, had come running into the bar.

"Foxy, Doris was in the parking lot! She's right on my tail!"

Foxy did what he had to do; he ran to the men's room at the back of the bar, barely making it in before Doris stormed through the front door. "Max, where is Foxy?"

Max, who had just taken over Foxy's stool, drink, and cigarettes, looked up and down the bar and back again.

"Gee, Doris, I don't see Foxy anywhere. Harry, do you see Foxy anywhere?"

"Hey, I don't see anything. I don't hear anything. I don't get involved in anything." This was the second lesson Jerry had been taught.

"Well, since when, Max, do you drink straight whiskey?"

"I love Seagram's straight," Max downed the rest of Foxy's drink and almost threw up on the spot. He was a good friend.

"And since when do you smoke Luckies?"

"Be happy, go Lucky," Max quoted the cigarette maker's slogan and lit a Lucky. Max didn't smoke.

"Ah-huh," Doris said, leaving the horribly coughing Max and walking toward the women's room, also at the back of the bar. The doors to both rest rooms were only about six feet apart. Doris stood between them with her back against the wall and waited.

Five minutes became 10 and 10 – 15. After almost 20 minutes, the door to Doris's right slowly opened and Foxy poked his head out of the men's room, only to be grabbed by the ear and literally pulled forcibly out the side door of the bar.

"Poor son of a bitch," another bar patron said.

"Don't worry about Foxy," Harry said. "He'll be back in an hour."

"Five bucks says he won't be."

"You're on."

Harry became five bucks richer when Foxy walked in 45 minutes later.

"Seven Mile Hub." In his dream, Jerry answered the phone on the eighth ring. The voice on the other end of the line was familiar.

"Hi Mom," Jerry said. "What's up?"

Jerry could actually see himself carefully listening to his mom on the other end of the line. He could also feel the earpiece of the phone against his ear and clearly hear his mom's voice as she spoke.

"Okay, Mom. I'll tell him. Yes, right away," Jerry said before hanging up with an overly loud click.

When Jerry walked out of the back room and headed behind the bar, all of the men grabbed their drinks and looked at him expectantly. Each one visibly relaxed and sighed with relief as Jerry walked silently past. As he approached the end of the bar, his dad turned to face his son: "Who called?"

"That was Mom."

"What she say?"

"Just that she wanted me to tell you that she's coming."

Harry smiled. "That's good."

# # #

Before falling asleep that night, Lucy took Harry's Army Air Corps photo out of her suitcase. She kissed the young man in the picture and simply said, "I'm coming," before putting it under her pillow with the torn dollar bill.

# # #

On the way to Petoskey the next day, Lucy refused to talk about what happened the night before.

"Mom, I wish you would tell me what you meant about my talking to Dad and Eddie. The whole thing is getting a little creepy."

"Jerry, there is nothing 'creepy' about it. There is just nothing more to talk about right now. You'll understand."

"That's like your telling me when I was a kid that I would understand things when I got older."

"Exactly, now tell me more about this woman you met, Edina, was that her name?"

Every time Jerry tried to broach the happenings of the night, days and decades before, Lucy would quickly and adeptly change the subject to Edina, his ex-wife, his childhood, past trips to Petoskey, when he had his tonsils out, the weather, anything. Finally, he gave up his efforts somewhere just north of Bay City. (Point to the webbing between your thumb and index finger, and you will be pointing to Bay City Michigan.)

Lucy had wanted to get an early start that morning and had called Jerry at 6 am to make sure they would be on the road by 7:30 'at the latest'.

At exactly 11:42 a.m., they crested the hill to see the turquoise splendor of Little Traverse Bay below.

"Oh my," Lucy said.

"Amazing, right Mom? That's one view that will never change."

Lucy sighed, knowing she was seeing eternity and that it was beautiful. "Can you take me to The Hub now?"

"Mom, maybe we should see if we can check you in at the Apple Tree first. I know it's a little early, but maybe the room will be ready."

"No, we don't need to check in. Let's just go to The Hub. That's why I'm here."

"But Mom, you know The Hub…"

"I know, I know. It's now the Shores condominiums."

"Yeah, I don't want you to be disappointed or expect something else."

"You've told me all that a thousand times, and for the thousandth time, I'm telling you that it doesn't matter."

"Okay, I will just shut up and drive."

"That's my good boy. Now, just wake me up when we get there. I need to take ten and rest my eyes."

When Anne and Jerry were growing up, 'taking ten' meant giving mom a break for a few minutes to catch her breath and maintain or regain her sanity. Resting one's eyes was a phrase that originated with Harry when Lucy's mom tried to switch TV channels from boxing to wrestling. "I'm not sleeping, just resting my eyes." Harry could 'rest his eyes' for hours.

As Jerry drove, Lucy closed her eyes and pretended to sleep. She didn't want to see all of the changes that had taken place in Petoskey over the years. Instead, she imagined that Aunt Clara's motel was still there at the bottom of the hill on the left, Wimpy's Hamburger shack was kitty-corner across the street on the right, and everything remained the same as it had been over 50 years ago when she last drove to The Hub with Harry.

Timing things perfectly, Lucy opened her eyes again when they were well out of town and driving through a rural landscape that hadn't changed much at all over the years. Lucy opened her window and breathed in the fresh northern Michigan air.

"I haven't felt so alive in years," she smiled. *So, so alive.*

After five minutes more, Jerry turned right into the parking lot of the Shores condominium complex, and Lucy Piasecki had a stroke.

Chapter 19

At first Lucy started slurring her words, she looked at Jerry with utter panic in her eyes. Then the headache started. After seeing what Harry went through, having a stroke had become Lucy's worst nightmare.

"Jerry, something bad is happening. Let's go to the hospital, real fast, okay?"

While it was difficult to make out the exact words Lucy spoke, their meaning was clear. Jerry peeled out of the Shore's parking lot and drove for his mom's life. He made the 15-minute trip from Crooked Lake to Northern Michigan hospital in under seven. By the time he got there his mom was unconscious.

Having made a frantic call to the hospital on his cell, Jerry found a doctor, a nurse, and several orderlies waiting for him at Emergency. He wiped a tiny bit of spittle that had bubbled from one corner of his mom's mouth, as the orderly opened the passenger door and put Lucy on the gurney.

It took several tries for the nurse to find a vein in Lucy's arm strong enough to hold the IV. Jerry ran alongside the gurney, holding his mother's other hand until they reached the ICU door."

"You'll have to wait out here," the doctor said. "I'll let you know what's happening as soon as possible. Our whole stroke team is here. We'll do our best."

Jerry kissed his mom's hand and placed it on her chest.

"We have to move fast, Mr. Piasecki," the doctor said. "Time is critical here."

"Go, go," Jerry choked out the words.

The doctor nodded to the attendants who picked up speed toward the ICU doors.

"Mom, please don't die," Jerry cried out as Lucy was wheeled through the doors to the Intensive Care Unit. He ran and looked through the narrow vertical windows, as his mom was wheeled down a long hallway. When the attendants made a right turn, leaving Jerry to stare down the empty hallway, he felt, no, he knew that his mom would soon be gone.

Jerry sat or paced in the ICU's waiting room for one hour, then two. He jumped each time the unit's door opened, and a doctor delivered news to someone else waiting for word on a loved one. Finally, after close to three hours, a different doctor than the one who had admitted Lucy walked into the waiting room and said out loud, "Mr. Piasecki?"

"That's me," Jerry jumped up from his chair and walked quickly to the man in white. "How's my mom?"

The doctor introduced himself as a neurologist named Dr. Kajowski. "I've just come from your mother. She regained consciousness almost as soon as we got her to ICU, and I have to say she's doing really well under the circumstances."

"Thank God."

"The CT didn't show any bleeding, although from all of the symptoms she had when she came in, we need to do a battery of tests to identify the blockage and figure out the appropriate treatment."

Jerry just kept hearing the phrase 'doing really well under the circumstances'. "So she's going to be alright?"

"As I said, we need to conduct more tests, but your mom is really tough. She's already complaining, saying she wants to leave."

"Can she?"

"No, again we need to wait for all the blood work to come back, and I want to run another scan in the morning. Then, my advice would be that we keep her under observation for a few days."

"Can I see her?"

"Not tonight. We gave her something to make her sleep."

And shut her up, Jerry thought.

"I'm sure she'll want to see you first thing in the morning."

# # #

"Get me out of here."

171

Those were the first words Lucy spoke as soon as Jerry walked in the door to her room the next morning.

"Mom, the doctor said you're demanding that they release you."

"Yes, I am. I know my rights, Jerry, and so do the doctors. They know they can't keep me here without my consent as long as I am coherent, and as you can tell I am as coherent as can be. Otherwise, they're holding me prisoner. Trust me, we talk a lot about this sort of thing at the home."

"Assisted living," Jerry corrected.

"The *home*," Lucy reiterated.

"Mom, you just probably had a stroke. You can't just waltz out of here like that."

"Well, Jerry, I am going to do just that."

"What did you see when we got to the Shores."

"That's what I have to find out. It all seems like a strange dream, the kind that you can almost remember, but then can't quite bring it back."

The splinter, Jerry thought.

"I just know that I need to go back there and that you need to take me there today. I mean right now."

"Mom, this is serious."

"I am serious."

Dr. Kajowski walked into the room with two nurses. "I hope you were able to talk some sense into this young lady."

"This *old* lady is full of *sense*," Lucy said. "I'm leaving."

"I really advise against it. Not enough time has gone by for us to be sure of what happened. We do know that you just had some sort of dramatic brain event…"

"You mean a stroke," Jerry said.

"Probably, yes, but we need to do more tests and keep your mother under observation for a few days to be sure."

"Mom?"

"Get this tube out of me right now."

When no one moved, Lucy dangled and then shook the arm with the IV in the direction of the nurses causing the IV stand to jiggle and the saline water in the bag to sploosh back and forth in time with her moving arm.

Dr. Kajowski looked at Jerry who nodded his head. The doctor in turn nodded to the nurses who moved forward to take out Lucy's IV and help her get dressed.

"You know you'll have to sign a paper that says that you understand that you're going against stated medical advice and that the hospital and doctors are not responsible for anything negative that happens to you."

Jerry gave one last hopeful glance toward his mom, but she had on her 'because I said so' face, so he knew there was no hope of convincing her to stay in the hospital where he felt she belonged.

One of the nurses helped Lucy to a sitting position on the bed and put her clothing next to her. "A little privacy?" Lucy looked at Jerry and Dr. Kajowski. "If you don't mind."

"Alright, Mrs. Piasecki," the doctor said. "Someone will be here with the papers for you to sign and a wheelchair."

"Can I roll her out?" Jerry asked.

"No, one of the nurses has to. You can meet her at the front entrance."

"See you there," Lucy said as the nurses closed the curtains around her bed. "Now, both of you—scoot."

Fifteen minutes later, Jerry waited in the Jeep at the front of the hospital. The nurse who had helped Lucy get dressed pushed the wheelchair to the curb. She and an orderly helped get her up from the chair and onto the front seat.

"Are you okay, Mom?" Jerry asked after hearing the click of his mother's seatbelt.

Lucy nodded. "Jerry would you mind driving up by Clara's for one minute before we head to The Hub. I want to see her place one more time."

That's gotta be the stroke talking, Jerry thought. *Doesn't matter.*

Jerry turned right out of the hospital and drove past the intersection of 131 and 31 and the Walgreens on the corner where Aunt Clara's motel used to be. Lucy just stared out the passenger side window as they went by the strip mall that once was the lime quarry. "Okay, she said. "Now, let's go to The Hub."

Jerry turned around in the Apple Tree parking lot. His mom seemed to be in a world only she could see and feel. "Mom, should I take you back to the hospital?"

"Why?" Lucy's voice sounded strong, even, in a way, young. "I'm fine. Let's go."

As Jerry stopped at the light at 31 and 131, Lucy smiled. "Isn't it wonderful! Just so wonderful!"

"What is mom?" The light changed to green and Jerry started to pull slowly through the intersection.

"How nothing has changed. It's all the same."

Jerry was convinced that his mom was having another stroke and, regardless of her protests, he intended to take her back to the hospital. "Mom, it's all different. Come on. Everything is different."

Lucy smiled: "Look in your rearview mirror."

"Why?"

"Just look."

As he drove past the bakery, Jerry looked in his mirror and saw the Petoskey Motor Court on the left and Wimpy's Hamburgers on the right.

Chapter 20

Jerry drove straight by the hospital and continued on toward, toward, *toward, toward what*; he didn't know. All thoughts of returning his mom to the hospital had disappeared.

The drive to Crooked Lake was a blur where past and present melted together in a hodgepodge of images both real and imagined. McDonald's was there, but evaporated into a mist which solidified into a forest.

Stafford's Bay View Inn looked the same, but as he drove by Jerry noticed that the parking spaces were filled by a DeSoto, two Nash ramblers, including one convertible, a Chevrolet Bel Air, and a Chrysler Imperial. There wasn't a Mazda, Hyundai, or Honda in sight.

A blaring car horn made Jerry quickly look at the road ahead, instead of at the parked cars. He managed to swerve back into his own lane, narrowly avoiding a head-on collision with a Studebaker.

What once was—was again, in a jumbled swirl of past and present that led to an undetermined future. Jerry drove by present-day stores and restaurants, but as he did, they seemed to jiggle and blur into stands of white birch trees, open fields, and homes from forgotten past lives and forever lost loves.

A green road sign with its white letters announcing '*Alanson 8 Mackinaw City 33'* was clear and remained solid. "We're getting close," Lucy said. "We're almost there."

Just outside Conway, Crooked Lake appeared on the right. "Look, the lake," Lucy's voice was filled with an excitement and strength Jerry hadn't heard in years. "Your father just loves that lake. You know, he once took me out on a little motor boat as the sun set. He pretended that the motor stalled out in the middle of the lake."

"What happened then?"

Lucy blushed. "He got it started again." There was a long pause and a little giggle. "About an hour or so later."

Jerry smiled and said nothing.

"The sky was so beautiful that night. You could see the Milky Way, and we counted shooting stars, making a wish on each one."

I wonder how many came true. Jerry thought.

"Such a beautiful, beautiful night," Lucy sighed.

As he drove, Jerry tried to keep his eyes on the lake as much as possible, in that way avoiding the ever-changing landscape around him. At least, the lake stayed pretty much the same as the miles went by. He would rapidly look back and forth from a full lake view, to a quick glance at the road just to make sure he was staying in his lane.

"We're here!" Now Lucy sounded young, anxious, and (Jerry thought) in love. "Turn, Jerry, turn. Turn here. Turn now!"

Jerry turned sharply to the right, immediately, hearing the distinct crunch of gravel under his tires as he left the road.

"Oh shit," Jerry found himself staring directly at a white house emblazoned with words announcing that they had arrived at *'THE HUB – Famous for Food'*

"We're here, Jerry. Finally here."

"I don't believe this. Mom, this can't be real." Jerry put his head against the steering wheel and closed his eyes.

"I love you, Jerry. Always remember that."

Without lifting his head from the steering wheel, it was Jerry's turn to respond: "I love you more."

As he spoke, Jerry heard the passenger door open and then quickly close. Lifting his head, he saw his mom walking toward the front of the car; Lucy Piasecki, again young, vibrant, and so very much alive.

"Mom?"

Lucy walked quickly toward the front door to The Hub, which suddenly opened. "Lucy!" Harry shouted, stepping out into the light. "Lucy, my Lucy!"

"Harry! My darling, my Harry!" Lucy started to run toward her husband.

176

Jerry watched as his father threw down his bar towel, ripped off his apron, and ran toward his bride.

A second or two later a hero and an angel embraced and kissed.

The kiss lasted a lifetime, a moment, an eternity. When their lips parted, Jerry could see them smiling broadly. In his mind, he heard his mother ask his father: "Will you always be there to catch me?"

He then heard his father's voice reply simply: "Always."

"Always?"

"Forever."

Holding hands and laughing, Harry and Lucy walked back into The Hub, pausing only for a moment for Harry to wave and for Lucy to blow her son a kiss goodbye.

Chapter 21

Jerry stared at the closed door of The Hub, unable to move until the building seemed to quiver and then glisten: almost becoming liquid, and then vapor before solidifying back into the Shores condominium complex. He looked to his right to see his mom's frail lifeless body in the passenger seat. Leaning over he ever so gently kissed her cheek before driving slowly back to Northern Michigan Hospital in Petoskey.

# # #

A week later, Jerry and Anne stood by their parents' gravesite; Section C, tier 9, space 28 at Mt. Olivet Cemetery on Six Mile and Van Dyke in Detroit. They looked down at the tombstone:

Harry R. Piasecki   Lucy S. Piasecki
Beloved Husband and   Beloved Wife and Mother
    Father
                    Love You Forever

Anne sighed deeply. "She was suffering so much toward the end. Maybe now, if anything comes after this life, maybe she really is back with Dad. Do you think so, Jerry? Do you think Mom's with Dad?

Jerry thought of telling Anne the whole story, but instead said: "I don't know the answer; but at least, now I know what I believe."

Epilogue

Several months later, Jerry woke up at 3 am. He remembered the dream; the one he had after dropping Rob off at the Pellston airport the day before he and Eddie had traveled to The Hub.

In the dream, his mom and dad were standing in a gray enveloping fog. They were distant but distinct. While they didn't actually talk, he heard them speak in voices more clear and beautiful than any he had ever heard before.

Harry and Lucy told their son that life is all lessons. Though things are critically important while we are living, after we leave, each smile, every tear, all experiences become just lessons learned.

"It's like a three year old trying to learn that two plus two equals four," Lucy said without speaking a word. "The lesson may be hard at first, but once learned, it is no longer difficult…it is just a lesson."

They both looked closely at their son: "We are all here to listen, to learn, and to love."

Now, these months later, Jerry remembered that the dream had ended when the fog engulfed his parents in an almost tender flash of light. He understood that he would not see them again.

Jerry knew he would remember the dream, and the message, forever. "Thank you," he said softly in the night. "Thank you, Mom. Thank you, Dad."

Taking a very deep breath, and then another, Jerry moved quietly over to the other side of the bed. Careful not to wake her, he kissed Edina's hair, again capturing its now familiar and ever enchanting scent. He whispered oh so softly into her ear, "I'll be loving you always."

CPSIA information can be obtained
at www.ICGtesting.com
Printed in the USA
BVHW041822280219
541463BV00016B/157/P